THIN AIR

LORE OF KING & SLATER BOOK 2

MATT ROGERS

Want more from Matt Rogers?

Watch or listen to my podcast, **"Heroic Traits,"** where I
break down life lessons from my novels:
https://linktr.ee/heroictraits

Follow me on Facebook:
https://www.facebook.com/mattrogersbooks

Follow me on Instagram:
https://www.instagram.com/mattrogersauthor

If you enjoy the book, make sure to leave a review! Your
feedback means everything to me, and encourages me to
deliver more books as soon as I can.

BOOKS BY MATT ROGERS

THE DANTE JACOBY SERIES

Be Somebody (Book 1)

Double Life (Book 2)

THE JASON KING SERIES

Isolated (Book 1)

Imprisoned (Book 2)

Reloaded (Book 3)

Betrayed (Book 4)

Corrupted (Book 5)

Hunted (Book 6)

THE JASON KING FILES

Cartel (Book 1)

Warrior (Book 2)

Savages (Book 3)

THE WILL SLATER SERIES

Wolf (Book 1)

Lion (Book 2)

Bear (Book 3)

Lynx (Book 4)

Bull (Book 5)

Hawk (Book 6)

1

L ife goes by fast.
Jason King's been contemplating this thought for months now, often during the loneliest stretches of his solo crusades through foreign war zones, when the sheer pressure of the isolation threatens to break him and he's forced to introspect just to keep his head on his shoulders.

Sometimes he forgets how quickly it passes.

It's important to remind himself, especially when the stress is overwhelming. Three years he's been doing this now. Three years and he's still breathing: he tries not to underestimate the magnitude of that achievement. It helps ease the mental burden, especially when he's thousands of miles from home and under constant threat of assassination and then remembers that he's only twenty-six years old and that most his age are aimlessly floundering through dead-end jobs this early in their adult lives.

Because that's when imposter syndrome creeps in.

I don't belong here, he starts to think when he's barely clinging to sanity behind enemy lines. *The military industrial complex has invested a small fortune in me. Do they know I still feel like a child?*

But he's alive.

It's a healthy reminder.

More than a thousand days of this unimaginable existence and now he's sitting at a beachside bar in Boca Raton with more than forty successful operations under his belt. He sips a beer as he watches the ocean lap at the golden shore, bronzed skin toasted by the sun. A five-star hotel looms behind him, overshadowing its attached beach club; soon the sun will set behind the extravagant tower and the lounges around him will cool in sudden shadow. King's formed a stellar routine over the course of his three-day stint in Florida: complete the necessary check-ins with Command in the mornings, drink beer slowly in the afternoons after punishing himself physically with self-imposed PT along the beach, then drink faster, with more urgency, as the sun dips low and the shadows of dusk begin to stretch.

Things could be much worse.

He figures it'll be another couple of days before he gets bored and starts itching for the end of the week's rest that his superiors mandated.

Then the bald man with the clear eyes walks into the beach club.

Mid-pull on his bottle, King takes one look at the newcomer and swallows a mouthful of beer with a grimace.

Life's about to get a whole lot faster.

"Clear eyes" might sound too vague to mean anything, but after three years spent interacting with the strange routines of the secret world, King's learned to spot a spook in milliseconds, and it's always the gaze that gives them away. The talented ones try to hide it — a predatory hyper-awareness of their surroundings — but certain tells are unavoidable. The bald guy's doing his best. He wears a pink linen shirt with the top three buttons undone, and white chino shorts; Birkenstocks on his feet. His tan is real, his posture laidback, the buzz of a couple of drinks lending him a certain swagger.

But as his eyes flash over the lounge, there's a tension in his pupils.

Underneath he's taut as steel.

He's good at masking it, but not good enough.

It's a formality when he saunters over to King and takes a stool on the opposite side of the table.

'Four-eight-one,' he says casually, then looks over his shoulder to make eye contact with a passing waiter and motion for a beer.

King slides an old-school Motorola pager from his pocket to check the numbers displayed on the small grey screen. It reads 481, but he already knew it would. He's never been wrong about clear eyes. He tucks the device away: three years in the covert world has taught him, above all else, that simple is best. A pager is so basic that if you encrypt it, there aren't any backdoors to be hacked. The only other person privy to the three digits — which automatically refresh every five minutes — is his chief handler Lars Crawford, so if the guy across from him knows them, he's solid.

King lowers his guard accordingly.

No one at the beach bar is in earshot of their table, so anything goes.

It's on the bald man to reveal how much he knows.

The guy looks King in the eyes: no bullshit, no nonsense.

He's a hard man. It's not like he's trying to hide his physique. A frame with the texture of concrete simmers beneath the bright shirt, and white scars cover his leathery forearms, permanently browned by years of sun exposure.

Probably desert sun, King figures.

'Allan Friesen,' the guy says.

King takes a final swig of his beer and stops the approaching waiter in his tracks by holding his empty bottle up. The waiter backpedals, fetches a second cold one, and brings both beers over for them. He pops the tops and withdraws with consummate professionalism.

Only then does King meet the bald man's gaze. 'Who's that?'

'Me.'

Friesen's expressionless. He almost looks bored.

King says, 'I'm—'

'I know who you are.'

'Right.' A long pause, strangely uncomfortable given the paradise that surrounds them. 'I don't know who left you out of the loop, but I'm under enforced rest, so—'

'Not anymore. We're going to Chile.'

It used to jar King badly when he heard he was being pulled back into the fray, like an electric shock to the central nervous system as he braced for the inevitable suffering. Those days are long gone. You get your life tipped on its head forty times over three years, and eventually it stops catching you off-guard. Constant chaos becomes the new normal. Downtime starts to feel like a cruel joke.

So King's not rattled.

If anything, he's relieved.

Business as usual.

But he still sighs. 'Why? What's happening in Chile?'

'Same as what's happening everywhere else,' Friesen

says with a shrug. 'But we're not going there to fight corruption. We could do that here. We're going because I was sent over as a location scout, and my trip proved successful.'

He waits for the follow-up question, which King refuses to provide. Friesen takes a long drink from his cold bottle and rolls his eyes.

'I found just the place to develop your skills,' he reveals.

A knot in King's guts. He'd almost prefer an op. 'Another training camp? How long?'

'A week, I'm told. Any longer than that and we'd just grind you into dust. Which benefits no one.'

King's no stranger to the literal hell of clandestine training camps. Without squadmates, the concentrated stints revolve entirely around him, pushing him to the brink and quite often tipping him over the edge. They reshape his meaning of "discomfort" and ensure that nothing in the field could ever take him by surprise. By the end of the nightmarish stretches, there are no levels of fatigue which can shock him, no physical sensations which can throw him off his game.

There's a reason that *"train hard, fight easy"* has become a cliché in combat sports.

Because it's true.

But it doesn't make the revelation any easier to digest. His insides tighten with dread. 'When do we leave?'

He doesn't bother making the gesture of saying "yes." It's a direct order; they both know he has no choice. He signed his life away three years ago in exchange for more money than he knows what to do with.

Even if he did, he doesn't have time to spend it.

'Tomorrow,' Friesen says. '0600. Homestead Air Reserve Base. Don't be late.'

He stands up to leave, taking his beer with him.

But something he said before was strange, and King can't suppress his confusion. Can't keep his mouth shut. 'A week?' he asks.

Looming over the table, Friesen raises an eyebrow, rolling the bottle's condensation over his leathery palm.

'Every camp,' King says, 'I ask how long. No one ever answers. No one ever tells me it'll grind me into dust. One time I asked why they keep me in the dark. I was told they don't like putting perceived limits on what I can do. Maybe they only think I can last a week. But if I don't know that, I might surprise myself. Might last eight days.' He eyeballs the spook. 'Why the sudden change of script?'

Friesen smirks. 'Because this time there isn't a fucking chance you'll last eight days.'

'We'll see.'

'You said "perceived limits." That's cute. Where we're going, there are hard limits.'

King falls quiet.

Friesen asks, 'You ever been twenty thousand feet above sea level?'

Shit, King thinks.

The dread mounts.

2

Allan Friesen steps out of the beach club onto a sidewalk drenched in sunset.

He tosses half his remaining beer in the trash.

The waiter tried to stop him leaving with the bottle, citing open container laws, but Friesen shot him a withering look and watched him squirm. He never wanted the rest of the beer. He just likes seeing the weak tremble. He lives for moments like those: when a lesser man makes a polite request but knows there isn't a damn thing he can do to enforce it.

Now Friesen pulls out a special phone — probably in the top ten most-encrypted devices on the planet — and speed-dials a number.

Lars Crawford answers without a word.

'All clear,' Friesen says. 'He'll be there: 0600.'

'Any pushback?' Lars asks.

'He's a little intimidated. He'd never show it, but I could tell. He'll dream of oxygen tonight. That's what you wanted, right? Keep his mind preoccupied, give him no room for suspicion...'

No answer.

'For what it's worth,' Friesen continues, 'I like him.'

'Nobody cares who you like,' Lars says. 'Just make sure he gets on that plane.'

The line goes dead.

L ars Crawford hangs up on Friesen and tucks his phone away.

He takes a deep breath.

Then, before he can psyche himself out, he throws the door open, moves through the whisper-quiet antechamber, and steps into the office of the man who runs the world.

Christian West — "The Golden One" — doesn't so much as glance up from his papers.

Maybe "running the world" is hyperbole, but that's the way it feels.

For the past three years, Lars has spent every waking moment of his life working himself to the bone in the name of "Black Force"; for West, it's a side project. Lars is lucky to catch a few hours of sleep a night before throwing himself back into the never-ending migraine of covert-ops intelligence; West often sleeps for eight or nine hours, wakes up, and immediately makes decisions that Lars would need to strategise for weeks to understand. "The Golden One" founded the most successful division in the history of deniable operations on a whim. He offhandedly gave Lars the green light when he observed a twenty-year-old Will Slater through a one-way mirror, then he went home and immediately cleared his mind to focus on broader issues.

Christian West is a different breed.

An automaton, a machine, a relentless marauder.

Barely human.

Every time Lars pays him a visit, it takes considerable courage just to walk through the door. But it's not like he has a choice. West thinks in thirty-year timelines, and if Lars even slightly delays his quest to shape his long-term vision, there's hell to pay.

Lars made the mistake of ignoring his superior's orders once.

Twice would prove fatal.

Finally, West looks up. Lars feels like he's been standing there forever, although it can't have been more than a few seconds. His face has flushed hot as if under the glare of a spotlight. He's like an ant in the sights of a mammoth magnifying glass, moments from incineration.

"The Golden One" says, 'Everything going to plan?'

What Lars wants to say is, *No, you evil piece of shit. Your plan, maybe: not mine. This world is my life, and you want to rip it all away from me as if it never existed at all. As if it never meant a thing. I wish I could leap over that desk and slash your throat.*

But he quite likes being alive, so what he actually says is, 'Yes, sir,' and then keeps his mouth shut.

West's blue-eyed stare bores across the expansive office. Lars wants to adjust his weight from foot to foot, but knows it'll look like squirming. He locks his knees and prays the blood doesn't drain from his head. He already feels faint. The room swims.

'Don't be bitter,' West says softly. 'It's unbecoming.'

Lars summons a little courage, which is no small feat. 'May I ask why?'

'You may ask,' West says with a mocking smile. 'I have no obligation to answer or tell the truth.'

'Of course. I understand.'

All quiet.

He's actually going to make me spell it out, Lars thinks. It hurts, and West must know it hurts, because the man is relishing it. With cerulean blue eyes, a long mane of black hair, and perfect white teeth, Christian West is everything Lars isn't: and not just looks-wise. There's a powerhouse of a mind between his ears, and coupled with his intense features, it's like he can reach out and pry whatever he wants from the very fabric of the universe. Like he can bend reality to his will.

He probably can.

Lars swallows hard. 'May I ask why you're considering shutting the program down?'

His life's work. His magnum opus. The crowning achievement of his career. All snuffed out because one man at the very top changed his mind.

'There's nothing left to *consider*,' West says. 'I've made the decision. It was an entertaining experiment, but it's done.'

Lars blinks, gulps back the crushing disappointment, and shifts his weight. "The Golden One" notices each of the three consecutive gestures. With each one, his smile inches a little further upward.

Lars understands that protest will achieve nothing, but he can't help himself. 'After the last two ops? King in Malta, Slater in Mozambique. You're seriously telling me you saw such spectacular results, back to back, and *that's* when you decided to nix it?' A pause, and then something darker takes over, and Lars no longer cares about his own wellbeing: all that concerns him is the excellence of his results. 'Honestly, Christian, what the fuck are you doing?'

Cold silence.

Christian West's gaze bristles and suddenly he's staring daggers.

Lars feels the immediate, overpowering need to put things right, if that's even possible. 'Sir, I'm sorry—'

'First-order consequences.'

Lars hesitates. 'What?'

'You only see first-order consequences. Jason King blasts his way through a terrorist cell in Malta, you see the bodies and think, *Good. Job done.* I see the bodies and all I can think about is the American bullets left in the heads of men who I know full well were funded by the same shell company that kicked money to certain corrupt members of the *Partit Nazzjonalista,* whose prime minster is currently in power. I expect the Labour Party to win the 2013 election, but walking that tightrope for the next three years is going to be both a diplomatic nightmare and a geopolitical clusterfuck.'

West stares.

Lars practically wilts.

'Sometimes,' West says, 'perfectly-executed brute force is no different from failure.'

Lars gets this. He's no fool. What he doesn't understand is why West authorised certain missions if he knew they would result in unfavourable outcomes. The briefings must have come across his desk — why had he let them through?

As if reading his mind, West says, 'Of course, we only clued in to the existence of that shell company after the fact. But it doesn't change what happened. You can walk back political decisions. You can't walk back bullets.'

The headache drilling at Lars' temples amplifies.

'You had a good run,' West says, both condescending and reassuring. 'My decision doesn't reflect on your abilities. You did an excellent job — I mean that. Otherwise I wouldn't let your insult go. So your reward is your life. Now get out of my office.'

Lars doesn't move. Voice small, he asks, 'Are you nullifying them all?'

West shrugs. 'What choice do I have? That's the name of the game. It comes with unique difficulties, though. I've let you fashion a small cohort of the world's best warriors: warriors I no longer have a need for. It goes without saying that anyone I select to take them out won't be up to par. So we'll start with King. Take him up to twenty thousand feet, tire him to the bone, then move in for the kill when he's physically destroyed. If it works, we'll give Slater the same treatment. And then the rest.' West sighs. 'I'll miss those first two, though. They're special. I mean that.'

Lars feels sick to his stomach. 'I know you do.'

West stares at him. 'Out. Go give the orders.'

Lars slinks out into the antechamber and makes the call.

'Yeah,' he confirms over the phone. 'Wait until he's dead tired. Then do it.'

4

King reaches the perimeter of the Homestead Air Reserve Base at 0559.

He's a stickler for punctuality.

In the muted hues of predawn, a gate guard takes one look at him and requests a three-digit number. In the form of an answer, King tosses him the Motorola pager: after this, he'll be in the constant presence of members of the secret world, and he no longer needs the ever-refreshing code.

The guard catches the device, stares at its small screen, and waves him through.

He ducks under the boom barrier and steps onto the base without getting pulverised by gunfire, which is a small victory. He's waiting for the day where he presents some cryptic proof of identity to a service member and is met only by a blank stare. It always feels like he's dreaming, floating through military installations like a nomad, drifting past uniformed soldiers who've all been briefed in advance and have to pretend he doesn't exist. His stint in a uniform was remarkably short, back before he was discovered by Lars

Crawford and swept into the shadow world. It already feels like a lifetime ago, a different universe.

Allan Friesen meets him at the edge of a vast runway.

The tarmac shimmers a ghostly blue in the strange moments before sunrise.

The pink shirt is gone. Friesen's clad in black khakis, thick Gore-Tex boots, and a rugged jacket that puffs up his considerable musculature like the Michelin Man. There's still nothing to identify him: King just assumes he's an officer with the Special Activities Center of the CIA, plucked from a Tier One unit after displaying remarkable, near-otherworldly abilities in the field. King was funnelled over from Delta Force three years ago in a similar transfer. Friesen seems the type to pounce on an opportunity like that.

The man doesn't offer a hand, just keeps his fists jammed in his jacket pockets. He looks permanently pissed off.

King gestures to the heavy layer. 'Little overdressed, don't you think?'

It's already over seventy degrees at dawn, and soon the summer heat will bake the tarmac.

'Winter in Chile,' Friesen grunts. 'Not like that matters anyway. At twenty thousand feet, it's always winter. Hope you brought a jacket.'

King wears a loose organic cotton T-shirt, size XXL, and faded jeans. Having secured his hair in a tight ponytail, he looks every part the wandering hippie, only with a physique forged in fire. In a rolltop backpack slung over one shoulder, he has a few changes of clothes: none designed for the cold. Outside of active operations, he lives like a hardcore mini-malist. His handlers provide all he needs for assignments.

'I—' he starts, but Friesen cuts him off with a sarcastic grin.

'You wouldn't even know where to look for the gear you need,' Friesen says; he means it to be biting. 'We've got you covered.' He looks over his shoulder. 'With me.'

King follows him down the runway to the lowered aft ramp of a Globemaster III military transport plane. The Boeing looms over them, shielding them from the sunrise.

They stride up into the cargo compartment: twenty feet wide, ninety deep.

The loadmaster nods to them as they pass by, then goes back to coordinating the pallets that workers are rolling up the ramp. Between the palletised cargo comes a pair of off-road jeeps, driven into the belly of the plane and secured beside the rolling tracks.

King takes a hard metal seat along one wall and stuffs his bag on the floor underneath. He watches the loading process with a certain admiration; he's come to love clinical efficiency in all its forms. The workers have a few tons of gear onboard in minutes, not counting the jeeps themselves, and then all the men disappear like they were never there at all.

King motions to the load as Friesen pulls down a nearby seat. 'Training camp on wheels?'

Friesen nods. 'Not a whole lot of pre-existing infrastructure on the side of a volcano.'

King stares blankly at the man. 'What?'

Friesen glances over as he secures his own harness. One eyebrow lifts slightly, then he smirks. 'Right. Didn't get to that part last night.'

'What are you talking about, a volca—?'

With the *stomp* of boots on echoing metal, heavy footfalls cut him off. King looks over to see a tall, lean man in his thirties stride up into the plane. The newcomer shares numerous features with King, but sports a few key differences. It's like looking in a strange, slightly distorted mirror. The guy wears his hair long, tugged back in a ponytail, and his eyes are blue ice. But he's more rugged — cheeks weathered, face relentlessly wind-battered — and there's more grey in his beard. It takes some serious effort to look more beat-to-shit than Jason King, especially after an operation like Malta, and his complexion betrays a brutal life spent savaged by the elements. The newcomer's also at least thirty pounds lighter than King, but he moves like a panther, all efficient motion and hyper-athleticism. His frame, hard as a rock, suggests every shred of muscle and sinew has been forged out of necessity.

But, despite a life of clear hardship, his eyes are warm and jovial as he surveys the cargo compartment. He seems to approach everything in jest because he's seen the bottom of the abyss.

King can relate, and likes him immediately.

The new arrival beelines for King with an outstretched hand, a gesture Friesen never bothered with.

'Mate,' the guy says, his British accent thick, 'did you ask what I think you just asked?'

King shakes his hand, just grateful for the presence of someone who actually communicates. 'I think they like keeping me in the dark.'

'Fuckin' pointless.' He side-eyes Friesen, doesn't offer a hand. 'Who're you, Grumps?'

Friesen doesn't answer.

The newcomer dumps himself down in the seat between them and faces King while securing his harness, as if Friesen doesn't exist. 'Well, I know you two are cut from the same cloth, but at least you look like you *enjoy* a beer, huh,

mate?' He jerks a thumb over his shoulder. 'Let me guess —
you met this wanker yesterday, he ordered a Budweiser or
some similar piss water, and drank it like he was angry that
he had to?'

King can't help himself; he laughs freely.

The prediction was so accurate, it's like the guy's psychic.

'Reece Evans,' the man says, jabbing a finger into his
own chest. 'You're Jason King?'

'Guilty.' King absorbs small details, like how effortlessly
Evans works the harness, as if complicated buckles are an
extension of his own hands. 'I take it you climb mountains.'

Evans grins. 'You're good. Yeah, I'm no spook. I do eight-
thousanders as often as I can afford it. For this job I'm a ...
well, what'd they call it? "Specialist advisor." They love their
fancy words, 'ey?'

'We're climbing a volcano?'

'Sort of. I'm here to make sure you don't stroll off a ledge.
I'd wager you're a rather valuable asset, mate.'

It's a relieving feeling to know that if King asks a question, Evans will answer it. 'And where might these
ledges be?'

Evans gets a flare in his eyes at the very thought of it, and
it certifies to King that the man is batshit insane.

You have to be, climbing *proper* mountains. In the realm
of "8000ers" — the fourteen peaks rising eight thousand
metres or more above sea level — you're effectively
spending your life savings to torture yourself half to death.

King understands the appeal.

'Ojos del Salado,' Evans says slowly, accentuating each
word as if the syllables are precious. 'The highest volcano
on Earth.'

5

Without fanfare, the aft ramp rises, and minutes later the Globemaster rumbles its way into the sky.

They're headed for Chile.

King watches Reece Evans look slowly around the shaking plane, taking in the jeeps and the pallets. The climber's gaze pans slowly over to King, and he says, 'This is all for you?'

'You said it. I'm a valuable asset.'

'Bloody hell.' A pause. 'They exploit you, I take it?'

Beside them, Friesen faces forward and says, 'Keep your mouth shut, Reece.'

Evans belly-laughs. Then he leans over and slaps Friesen on the shoulder. It's such a ballsy gesture that King feels immediate, unwavering respect for the climber. Evans isn't from this world, but he's not an idiot, and he must know he's playing with fire.

He knows; he just doesn't care.

'Mate,' Evans says to Friesen, 'you got any idea the sheer

volume of NDAs they made me sign? Maybe if the gloves were off you'd squash me like a bug, but for this gig ... I'm untouchable, yeah? They specifically tracked me down and hauled me in for this. You ... you're replaceable. They could put any grumpy squaddy in your place.'

Friesen's glare is pure rage, but he doesn't make it physical, which proves, above all else, that Evans is onto something.

'What's your point?' Friesen asks slowly, through gritted teeth.

'If we wanna talk pay,' Evans says just as slowly, 'we'll talk pay. There's only one person on this plane who's gotta keep their mouth shut. It ain't me, and it ain't the guy this little excursion was built around.' He turns back to King. 'So ... they exploit you?'

King doesn't mind the tension; he began thriving in chaos a long time ago.

In his world, it's wrong if everything's going right.

'No,' he admits. 'I have a ... unique relationship with the brass.'

Evans smiles warmly, and it's genuine, which makes King like him even more. It's a rare thing to find someone who's genuinely happy for you when you share good news. He's learned that envy can be the most destructive of the seven deadly sins.

'Good for you, my friend,' Evans says. 'I'll get there one day. I'm sure of it, mate...'

He stares vacantly into space, and King sees that money is the impossible puzzle that controls the man's existence. For a man as free-spirited as Evans, the lack of control must be a physical pain.

'You said you were untouchable,' King says. 'Surely that means you can command a decent fee.'

'Doesn't quite work like that. This is a once-off. It's unique. And there are a handful of crazy bastards like me they could turn to if I said no. So my leverage is jack-shit.' Evans gives King a curious sideways glance. 'You must be the craziest bastard of them all, if you can demand whatever money you want.'

'There are others,' King admits, aware of Friesen's thunderous stare. But he doesn't care about disclosing sensitive information; Evans is sworn to secrecy, and it's the only conversation that King can have on the plane without feeling like he's talking to a brick wall. At the very least, it's refreshing. 'There are men like me. Maybe women, too. I wouldn't know. I've never met them.'

'You play the solo game?'

'That's the job.'

'If you can list your demands, mate,' Evans says, 'then that's some job. I'm jealous.'

'You wouldn't be if you knew what it involved.'

After a beat of silence — if you could call the dull roar of plane engines "silence" — he looks over and finds Evans staring at him. There's a manic glint in the climber's wide-eyed gaze.

'What?' King asks.

'Don't make the mistake of thinking you're the only psycho alive.'

King hesitates. 'I don't think that.'

'You do, mate, whether you want to admit it or not. I'm sure you put yourself through hell, but loonies like us ... well, we do that, too, whether rewards are guaranteed or not. They haven't told me anything, but I take it you're gifted in some way. Maybe you're smart as fuck. Maybe you react like lightning. Whatever it is, you don't give it enough credit. I'm sure you work like a demon, but you think you work harder

than everyone else. Let me tell you, pal — you ever voluntarily put yourself on an eight-thousand metre peak, genetic
gifts don't mean shit. Underneath, we're all just fragile skin
and bone.' He pauses. 'The mountain makes cowards of us
all.'

King might have rebuked the insult, but three years in
covert operations have taught him humility, so all he says is,
'I'm guessing that's what I'm here to learn.'

Evans says nothing for a beat, chewing a cracked lower
lip. Then he wags a finger as he cocks his head to one side.
'Well, who knows, mate? Maybe you *are* special.'

'Why?'

'I've met soldiers,' Evans says simply. 'That was an ego
test, just then.'

'You thought I'd snap?'

Evans doesn't answer. King knows the way he handled
the conversation has thrown the climber off so viscerally
that it's made the man reconsider everything he thought
about those in uniform (not that King ever wears a uniform.)

'Well, you nailed it,' King admits. 'I have close to the
fastest reaction speed on earth. But by now we're over forty
ops in, and I'm still here. Gifts only take you so far. Sooner
or later, advantages chew you up and spit you out.' He
hunches forward in his seat, closer to Evans. 'You want to
know why I'm still alive?'

'Yeah,' Evans says, and it's genuine, passionate. 'Yeah,
mate, I do.'

In that moment, something invisible connects them, and
a man like Allan Friesen will never understand. King and
Evans are two psychos in a mad world, lacking anything
resembling ego.

They are free to be mad.

King looks the climber in the eyes. 'Because I train like I have the worst reaction speed on earth and need to make up for it.'

Evans grins. 'Oh, we're gonna have some fun up there.'

6

T he next eight hours pass in a silence that becomes monastic.

King's found that's usually the way it goes. He's been shepherded onto a military transport plane more times than he cares to admit, often with guests like Reece Evans: men from a different world, brought on in special circumstances. But once that initial excitement fades, reality sets in and everyone steadily clams up.

Friesen was mute from the get-go, and nothing changes as the hours drag.

King and Evans settle in their seats, the cargo compartment gets freezing, and the roar in their ears begins to batter them into submission. They drift in and out of uneasy sleep, despite the fact that both their lives are built around uneasiness.

Some things you never get used to.

When they touch down at five p.m. local time, the aft ramp rumbles down to reveal an endless, sweeping desert stretching past the runway to melt into the horizon. A biting wind howls, and all King can see is desolation. It's winter, only forty or fifty degrees: a world away from summer in Florida. The land is barren, dreary, and oppressive dry.

The emptiness is ominous.

'Never been to Chile,' King says to no one in particular, only intent on filling the strange quiet.

Evans is already jogging down the ramp, out of earshot, but Friesen pulls up beside King.

'This is *Aeropuerto Copiapó,*' the spook says. 'It serves a small city — Copiapó, you might have guessed — out here in the Atacama desert. The volcano we're using to host this expedition sits right on the Argentina-Chile border. It's a five hour drive, or thereabouts. I made it last week while scouting — it's rough. We won't be there until the dead of night, but we'll need to drive up to camp regardless. That's another reason we chose this location: due to the sensitivity, we need to head in and out fast, and the trails up the volcano allow for jeeps to get up above six thousand metres. Some Chileans tried it three years ago and succeeded. I think they broke a record in the process, the mad bastards.'

'We're driving up in the dark? Why the rush?'

Friesen opened the floodgates, and now he's forced to provide the intel he held back for so long. Wearing a grimace, he relents. 'Our bosses have certain privileges in Argentina, which is the only reason this visit is even permissible. Half of Ojos del Salado sits in Argentina, after all. But I'm told the same favours don't extend over the border. We only landed here 'cause it's the fastest way there, but the Chileans don't know much about what we're doing here. There's no reason to suspect a threat, but it pays to stay frosty. Especially with such a *valuable* asset to babysit.'

The last sentence drips with sarcasm.

King takes one look down the ramp to check that Evans is out of sight. When the loadmaster and the co-pilot emerge from the door leading through to the cockpit, King turns and points a finger back the way they came.

They get the message and scurry away.

Friesen watches. 'Think you're a tough guy, huh?'

King offers no explanation.

He just steps into range, inciting an immediate reaction from the spook. Even civilians don't like their personal space crowded, let alone a trained killer like Friesen. The spook goes for the obvious line of defence, which is pure offence. He tries a violent two-handed shove, exploding off the mark in an attempt to take King by surprise, and if he succeeded it might have delivered a debilitating case of whiplash to his priceless asset.

But he makes the same mistake they all do, even the ones who know King is fast.

Because until you see it in the flesh, you'll never understand *how* fast.

King sees the shove coming and pivots at the hips. He snatches Friesen's meaty left forearm out of thin air, and as he rotates he knocks the limb aside. The momentum smashes one of the man's hands against the other and he stumbles sideways involuntarily, all his righteous anger working against him as he loses balance. Before he can right himself, King surges in even closer, making the angles all awkward. Friesen tries to rotate back but King yanks an arm around his throat and drags him back off his feet so he slumps in an unresisting heap on his rear. King locks in the rear-naked choke with the unconscious expertise of a third-degree Brazilian jiu-jitsu black belt.

The speed seems to defy physics.

Allan Friesen, probably feared all throughout the Special Activities Center and the CIA at large, is rendered useless in half a second. He tries to writhe his way out, but each bout of resistance is met by King cinching the choke tighter, and when the man's head turns purple and veins throb grotesquely at his temples, he concedes defeat and taps twice on King's forearm.

In the world they inhabit, tapping means a whole lot more than mere submission.

Out here in the lawless desert, at the very fringes of civilisation, it's admitting, *You can kill me. Whenever you want, you're capable of killing me.*

King knows the ego sting is physically painful.

He's been in Friesen's shoes before.

A long time ago.

He lets go, but doesn't help the spook to his feet. Friesen clambers upright, boots echoing on the metal ramp. The time it takes him is intensely noticeable. In each millisecond, it's as if King is saying, *Right there, I could kill you again.* Over and over and over. When he's finally on his feet, which takes no time at all but feels like an eternity, they face off again, but it's all different now.

The dynamic has crystallised, and is now obvious to both parties. There's no longer any room for debate, no *what-ifs*.

In a fair fight, one on one, with no weapons…

…King would crush him like a bug.

But Friesen is undeterred.

'Careful,' the man says quietly as the Globemaster's engines power down. 'I'm responsible for your safety until we're over the border.'

King eyes him, daring him to make good on the threat. 'You think you're the first to try to sell me out?'

A wry smile. 'Oh, I'm not selling you out. Not even close.'

He turns and walks down the ramp.

The howling wind lifts the tension and carries it away.

7

By the time the loadmaster backs the jeeps, one by one, out onto the tarmac of the desert airport, there's an uneasy truce in the air.

If that's what you'd call it.

King loiters in the cargo compartment to give both himself and Friesen some breathing room, and also to study the pallets that come rolling past on their tracks after the jeeps have been reversed out of the plane. He checks that Friesen's nowhere in sight, then steps in front of the first pallet, forcing the loadmaster and co-pilot to grind it to a halt before they hit the ramp.

King nods his silent thanks as he opens a certain container and removes a piece of equipment, which he packs in his own bag before shooing the crew along.

You can never be too careful.

Then he strolls down the ramp like nothing's amiss.

Once the pallets are out on the tarmac, Friesen distracts himself from his own ego and sets to work distributing an arsenal of equipment between the vehicles. That takes up enough of his concentration to move on from the physical altercation, and by the time he orders the loadmaster and co-pilot behind the wheels of the jeeps — who, it seems, are now their drivers — it's like it never happened at all.

Which doesn't fill King with confidence — he doubts it's water under the bridge — but it's better than the alternative of keeping the tension front and centre.

Well, we're here now, the truce seems to say. *Let's not waste the trip.*

Evans had sensed that something went down between the two of them and stayed resolutely out of the way as the jeeps were loaded. Now, when Friesen makes for one vehicle, Evans beelines for the other. King goes to follow the climber, but Friesen calls out: 'No. With me.'

It's actually reassuring. King's got a SIG Sauer P226 in an abdomen holster, and it'd be a hell of a lot easier to blow Friesen's brains out from behind than shoot at him from another vehicle.

Not that it would come to that, King reminds himself.

Maybe it's wishful thinking.

He'd very much like to leave South America alive; perhaps his love of life is clouding his judgment, making him too optimistic.

But he gets in the rear seat, behind Friesen in the passenger seat.

They peel away into the parched Chilean desert.

8

I t's like they flew to Mars.

Every picture King's seen of the Red Planet is mirrored here, from the flat arid plains, to the merciless dryness, to the alien atmosphere in the freezing air. The small convoy — just the two open-topped jeeps loaded with weatherproof cases taken from the pallets — barrels south until the desert changes suddenly, presenting to them the small mining city of Copiapó.

There's a museum, a university, a mall, a couple of parks, and a sea of residential housing, but against the backdrop of such a hostile landscape, the place has the feel of a fake model town built to test nukes.

King shifts uncomfortably in his seat as they rumble down the city's central avenue. Locals by the roadside stop whatever they're doing to stare; he doesn't blame them. They're barely concealing the small arsenal of weaponry on board, and the Chileans aren't stupid: one look at the giant cases and the gear and they'll put two and two together.

He leans forward in his seat, closer to Friesen's ear to

compensate for the wind. 'What privileges do we have in Argentina that don't extend over the border?'

'That's complicated,' Friesen calls back, 'and need-to-know.'

'Then you aren't aware of *my* privileges,' King says. 'If I ask something, it means I need to know.'

'You always this much of a prick?'

'I match the energy of whoever I'm speaking to.'

Friesen can't help himself; he scoffs. Then his walls come down. He's made things as difficult as they can be without causing an actual incident, so he must deem it time to back down and answer — especially after the chokehold. 'A few government cronies in Argentina are in hot shit. They've been making shortsighted decisions for a few years now. Our boss saw where it would lead — he's good at that — and stepped in to help them out before they realised he only did it for leverage.'

'Shortsighted decisions?'

'Economic bullshit. They've been manipulating the statistics since 2007. Trying to trick the people into thinking inflation's lower than it actually is. Don't ask me how it works — I don't mess with politics. I just shoot who I'm told to shoot. Keeps things simple. I'm sure you're on the same page.'

'I can wrap my head around inflation,' King says. 'I appreciate the concern, though.'

Friesen holds back a retort, then presses on. 'Yeah, well, our boss noticed them cooking the books a while back, saw how bad it was going to get, and offered to buy a few hundred million worth of government bonds linked to inflation. Bottom line: they now owe him a boatload of money that he never expected to get back anyway. So if he says he's sending some friends over for an all-access training camp, they roll out the red carpet ... or their economic situation comes to light.'

'A few hundred million,' King repeats. 'That's a lot of leverage.'

Friesen nods, but says nothing else.

King stews in thoughts that verge on paranoia. If you wield that kind of influence, you can ask for a whole lot more than permission to slap a few operatives on the side of a mountain. If the country's economy is propped up on a house of cards, and you own those cards ... well, your power's virtually limitless.

'You said "our boss."' King stares at the back of Friesen's head. 'You mean Lars Crawford?'

He catches a sliver of Friesen's smirk as the soldier faces forward.

'Lars Crawford has a boss,' Friesen says. 'Everyone you know, everyone you've ever interacted with ... they all have a boss.'

'Even you?'

'Especially me.'

'You got a little more information for me?'

'Now *that's* need-to-know.'

'I told you—'

'I know what you told me,' Friesen says bluntly. 'I'm sure you could knock my head off my shoulders if you really wanted. But compared to the hornet's nest you're poking, that's nothing.' The spook looks over his shoulder, meeting King's gaze for the first time since they stepped off the plane. 'Know your place. It's for your own good.'

King doesn't reply; something in Friesen's tone disturbs him. He gets the sense he's caught a peek behind the curtain. He doesn't like what he sees. It feels as if he's treading water in the middle of the ocean, with no concept of the depth beneath his feet. If he slips under the surface, he might plummet for miles…

Friesen slaps the driver on the shoulder and says, 'Here.'

The man hits the brakes and the jeep screeches to the shoulder on the far side of the city. They stop beside a dingy taqueria food truck serving Peruvian food to passing traffic.

'Grab a bite,' Friesen says. 'I got a call to make, and you'll thank me later. It's MREs from this point out.'

'A call?' King asks. 'You standing down the attack dogs? Too risky to hit me in Chile now?'

He's only half-joking.

Friesen doesn't grace him with a response, just works a bulky sat phone as he pops the passenger door and strides hard and fast away from the jeep.

King meets Evans in front of the food truck.

The climber gives him a strange look. 'I heard the tail end of that.'

'I wasn't serious,' King replies, unsure if he's being truthful.

'Mate, if I've walked into the middle of a civil war…'

'We're spooks,' King says. 'Off the books. Deniable. We use that sort of humour.'

'Uh-huh.' Evans' eyes drift left to where Friesen stands fifty feet from the jeeps, hunched over against the wind, deep in inaudible conversation with someone on the other end of the line. He looks back at King. 'Just keep an eye on him. I don't trust him one fuckin' bit, and I don't know the first thing about this world. Maybe I'm wrong.'

'Yeah. Maybe.'

King turns to the sliding window of the dormant food truck and a face pops up right in front of him, so sudden it jackhammers his heart in his chest.

9

I t's a kid.

Eight, nine years old.

A mess of black hair, bushy eyebrows, caramel skin.

He stands on his tiptoes and stretches as tall as he can manage to slide the taqueria's window open. It's still an effort; his stubby fingers tremble and his jaw clenches in determination. But he manages.

'Hello!' he shouts, beaming with joy. 'It is the nice to meet of you!'

King exchanges a glance and a small smile with Evans, then turns back to the kid. 'Hello. What's your name?'

'David!' the boy shouts again, as if every time he tests his English it needs to be at the maximum possible volume. 'I am the boy of food! I want your telling with what you want of eat!'

King eyes the menu and sees a pork and potato sandwich. He figures he'll need the carbs. '*Pan con chicharrón,*' he reads.

Evans says, 'Make it two.'

'*Two pan con chicharrón!*' the boy cries, almost ecstatic. 'I give to the order of my mother! She do the cook!'

King's quietly relieved that David isn't single-handedly running the food truck. The boy grits his teeth and furrows his brow as he memorises the seemingly complicated order, then he turns to run away. But he fixates on the jeeps, then looks at King. 'You are of the soldier and the guns?'

Evans points at King. 'He is.' Then jabs at himself. 'I'm not. I'm boring.'

'*Ha!*' David yells, and vanishes as quickly as he appeared.

Once they're alone, King shakes his head softly. 'If that happens again, stay mute. Kid doesn't need to know something like that.'

He thought the climber would fall into line, but Evans rolls his eyes. 'Oh, yeah — it's *such* a mystery what we're doing here.'

King doesn't push it. Evans is his only ally.

David's mother — in her thirties, round and plump with beet-red cheeks — materialises at the window five minutes later and hands them two pork and potato sandwiches with a smile and a nod. Either she speaks less English than her son, or she's embarrassed to try.

'David,' King says, pointing over her shoulder. 'Very clever.' He taps the side of his head to make his point.

She beams and nods vigorously.

Evans hands her some crumpled bills — far more than the listed price — and she bows a gracious thanks. They gorge on the *pan con chicharrón* as they move away from the taqueria, meeting Friesen back at the vehicles.

He takes a single disgruntled look at them. 'It's fine — take all day.'

In response, King bites into the bread roll even slower.

'You're the one who stopped to call off the hit,' he mumbles, mouth full.

'*Enough,*' Friesen hisses. 'It doesn't even sound like you're joking anymore. Get in the fucking jeep.'

King clambers across the rear seats.

I was never joking, he thinks as they surge away from Copiapó into the cold desert.

10

The jeeps leave civilisation behind.

Copiapó falls away and they plunge east into a rocky wasteland, barrelling for the Argentinian border. Far on the horizon, a mountain range looms, so enormous it doesn't look real. Between the jeeps and the high plateau lie a sea of dry river valleys cutting through the desert.

King barely notices the landscape; he's stewing in thought.

He can't take his mind off what Friesen said before.

'Our boss noticed them cooking the books a while back, saw how bad it was going to get...'

The spook said it so casually, as if it was no big deal. But it is. A few hundred million in bonds would be priceless to a financially distressed government, and if someone in the upper echelon predicted this years in advance...

It's genius.

King knows his handler, Lars Crawford. Knows him well. The brains behind Black Force, Lars demonstrates flashes of brilliance, occasional moments of pure genius, but never outside the realm of deniable operations. The covert world is his domain, and King knows Lars specialises at the cost of everything else, personal life included. He doesn't scheme on the international stage, doesn't concern himself with anything but the abilities of his operatives. All he cares about is how to best sharpen his swords.

It's paid off — sometimes King can't believe what Lars' program has shaped him into — but it only confirms what Friesen already said.

That there's someone higher.

The real shot caller.

He knows it's pointless to speculate who the man might be. If he hunts for answers, he'll never get them: in three whole years, he's only ever learned what the upper echelon deemed it necessary for him to know. He understands his place. He may be the most effective assassin in government history, but that still makes him a foot soldier, no matter how talented. He doesn't think in decade-long timelines. Doesn't plan the jobs.

Just accepts them.

And he's okay with that.

So, although it's difficult, he forces all the questions from his mind and focuses on the terrain. The desert is so vast and remote that gazing at the horizon is like a form of meditation. His thoughts go quiet.

Staring out the window makes him feel insignificant, and not in a bad way.

Travel, he's come to learn, is the ultimate perspective changer. Over forty operations, he's now visited twenty-two different countries across six of the seven continents. Sure, he's not exactly strolling around with a map and a list of popular tourist spots — usually he's fighting for his life against small extremist subsections of these countries' respective populations — but the experiences have none-theless shifted his worldview.

He's seen so much of the planet, especially its harshest and most inhospitable places.

It means that when he's home, he takes nothing for granted. If his ego ever runs away from him, all he has to do is take one look around and see that he's just a tiny speck in the grand scheme of things.

Maybe it's too philosophical for someone who smashes heads together for a living.

He doesn't care.

One of his favourite quotes is by the Athenian general Thucydides: *"The society that separates its scholars from its warriors will have its thinking done by cowards and its fighting by fools."*

He's never forgotten it.

Now the sun melts away as one hour blends into two, and although the sky lags behind, it doesn't take long for the last of the light to extinguish. The darkness seems greedy as it swallows the desert plains. Then there's nothing but the twin sets of jeep headlights and the never-ending black. The suspension rattles and jolts underneath King as the road grows steadily worse. All thoughts on philosophy are gone now, replaced by heightened awareness. Every shadow is a threat, and Friesen's unmoving silhouette up front sets him on edge.

But nothing happens.

No ambush.

King stares at the back of the soldier's skull and desper-ately wishes he could read the man's thoughts.

The night masks all reference points, and the only way to know they're starting the climb up to the high plateau is from a slight weight on King's chest, pressing him gently against the seat back as the jeep tackles the incline. They ascend for what feels like hours, and finally stop at a remote customs checkpoint to sort documentation with an official who must have been summoned in the dead of night.

While Friesen handles their business, King steps out of the jeep to find his vision swaying. He sees stars and has to grip the door just to steady himself. Once the dizzy spell clears, he checks his rugged hiking watch.

It reads *10,850.*

Ten thousand feet of elevation puts them in the same ballpark as Leadville, Colorado. King visited the former mining town two years ago to run its annual hundred-mile ultramarathon under a fake name. Back then, at the tail end of his first year as a covert operative, he felt invincible, and figured one of the hardest endurance events in the country would be a nice vacation between assignments. The Leadville 100 climbs and descends fifteen thousand feet in total; he thought nothing of it. When he finally stumbled across the finish line after twenty-eight hours, lungs burned raw and coughing blood, he weighed seventeen pounds less than when he started. He promised to never underestimate altitude again.

Surviving that ordeal was what gave him quiet confidence for this camp, but now he looks around and tamps down the tendrils of panic.

Because ten thousand feet is now a warm-up.

Evans walks up to him in the dark, and it only takes the climber a moment to see the look in King's eyes and know what he's dealing with: fear of the unknown.

Evans clamps a hand down on his shoulder. 'We just shot up to three thousand metres like a cannonball, mate. Don't freak out if you're woozy. It'll pass.'

King peers up into the pitch black, and swears he can see the outline of tremendous peaks against the night sky.

'I take it we're not doing any acclimatising,' he says.

'Nah,' Evans replies quietly. 'I can't lie — above five thousand metres, it's gonna get rough. I guess that's the point, though. I warned against it, but they don't want us taking our time.'

King eyed the climber. 'You'll handle it fine?'

'I'll handle it like you're gonna handle it. Just 'cause I've been at altitude before, doesn't make it any easier to deal with. Doesn't work that way. Especially if there's no acclimatisation.'

'So what do you do?'

'Huh?'

'When you start feeling like shit?'

Evans grins in the faint glow of the headlights. 'Enjoy it.'

He swaggers back to the other jeep.

11

They gun it for another couple of hours across sand flats and up steep, snowy slopes.

The air gets ever colder, ever thinner.

King throws on another Gore-Tex layer and hunches against the wind, which has turned vicious. Friesen remains ramrod straight, literally ignoring the elements, and King can't shake the feeling that the spook is far tougher than the altercation in the plane would suggest. It reminds him of what Evans said: *'You think you work harder than everyone else.'* Maybe the climber is right; maybe King mistakes talent for hard work. It eats at him like a parasite of doubt, because it could be true.

Perhaps he can only overpower other soldiers because of genetic gifts.

What if, in every other arena, Allan Friesen is superior?

Then those doubts fall away as they climb higher still — suddenly all he can focus on is his laboured breathing and the drilling pain behind his eyeballs.

He checks his watch: *15,900.*

They're close to the altitude that Evans warned about.

Screaming toward the dreaded five thousand metres.

And it's hell. No other way to put it: it's pure suffering. With proper acclimatisation — climbing during the day, sleeping lower at night — there would have been no issue, but now King can't catch a full breath and his headache is a savage migraine and his guts churn with the *pan con chicharrón* he ate four hours ago. As they bounce and rumble through the freezing night, King squeezes his eyes shut and wonders if there's any point to this.

They may as well have just kept him in Florida and hit him fifty times in the head with a baseball bat.

It's some consolation when he opens his eyes and spots Evans sticking his head out of the jeep up front, vomiting a geyser of pork, potato and bread from the moving vehicle. In front of King, Friesen observes the bout of puking wordlessly.

King taps him on the shoulder, head pounding. 'You're good?'

Friesen doesn't turn around. 'I scouted this spot last week, remember? Got a bit of acclimatisation there.'

'How long were you here?'

'Just a day.'

'Did you feel like this when you first came?'

'Worse.'

At least that's something. At face value, the science doesn't seem to make sense, but King's no expert and forgets it. He couldn't dwell on it if he wanted. All his conscious effort is focused on not throwing up the *pan con chicharrón.*

Twenty minutes of hellish off-road driving later, they're there.

Wherever "there" is.

All King sees is more limitless darkness as the jeeps coast to a halt on a featureless sand flat. He stumbles out onto solid ground, woozy and laboured, and the moment he straightens up he loses control of his stomach and vomits bitterly into the grey sand. Pale and sweating, he rights himself and wipes his lips. An invisible vice tightens on his temples, the pressure seeming to mount with each second that passes.

He peers out into the abyss, past the headlights, and sees something very strange. It looks to be a shipping container, painted orange, that serves as some sort of remote mountain hut.

He gestures to it wordlessly; his confusion speaks for itself.

'This is the Atacama Refuge,' Friesen explains. 'That hut is called Refugio Rojas. A ranger lives there in the climbing season.'

'Are we in the climbing season?'

'Hell no. We're on our own.'

It checks out. The container looks abandoned, and the drivers set to work hauling tent bags out the back of the jeeps. They begin setting the tents up in the hard sand around the hut as a bout of gale-force wind rips across the plain, complicating their efforts. King notices the oxygen tanks the drivers lug around, both of them inhaling occasionally from dangling masks to dissipate the effects of altitude. He doesn't bother asking for a hit. There isn't a chance he'll be afforded the same luxuries.

He barely has the energy to remain upright. His muscles have turned to lead, his own bulk dragging him down like a deadweight instead of aiding him. He understands now why Evans is so thin. In the climbing world, if you want to be any good, it's a necessity.

Evans approaches him as the drivers wrestle with the tents nearby.

'You look okay,' Evans says.

The discomfort makes King brutally honest. 'I feel like complete shit.'

A nod. Even the climber looks unsteady on his feet from such a rapid and unrelenting ascent. King checks his watch for the final time that night: *17,240*. He grimaces. It's above five thousand metres, above where Evans said the real punishment would begin.

King struggles to hold it together as he jerks a thumb over at Friesen, who's out of earshot. 'He's fine.'

'Yeah,' Evans says quietly, observing the spook. 'Something's up with that.'

'What do you mean?'

'He must have been here for a while before. Wonder what he was up to.'

'Only a day, he told me.'

Pale in the headlights, Evans smiles sardonically and shakes his head. 'Impossible. At minimum, it'd take a few to see lasting benefits.'

'Why would he lie?'

King knows how ridiculous the question sounds, but the thin air is frying his brain. He desperately hopes a night's sleep brings some meagre improvement.

Evans just stares. 'You tell me, mate.'

The driver of the other jeep signals that the climber's tent is ready, and Evans stumbles away without another word.

King stands there in something of a fugue state until his driver raises a hand, having finally wrestled the tent together. It could have taken minutes or hours; King completely lost track of time. He drags his sleeping bag and stainless steel water bottle over, pretty much falls into the tent, and barely manages to work the sleeping bag free before he collapses atop it, in similar fashion to how he finished the Leadville 100.

He doesn't really sleep.

Just lies there, heart pounding over a hundred beats per minute as his body fights to absorb oxygen that doesn't exist. He can tell that what little remains in the air is barely enough to keep him afloat. Recovery is a forgotten concept, and he figures that's what his superiors are going for.

But paranoia festers, and he wonders whether it's to test how he operates in horrendous conditions, or to simply get him so tired that he can't fight back.

He catches a few interrupted bouts of light sleep, punctuated by bad dreams.

Nightmares of knives in his back.

12

Allan Friesen waits for quiet to settle over the base camp.

Well, "quiet" is relative: there's nothing quiet about gale-force winds.

But when Jason King and Reece Evans disappear inside their tents and there isn't so much as a peep of movement for the next ten minutes, that's when he knows. They may not be asleep, but they've brought their guards down and tuned the world out, and all Friesen will see from their side of the camp for the rest of the night is the rippling of canvas.

He rounds to one side of the ranger's hut, using its heavy bulk as wind protection, and dials a number on his sat phone.

Lars Crawford answers, voice tinny against the gales that whistle around the sides of the container.

'How's he doing?' the handler asks.

Friesen doesn't sugar-coat it. 'He's fucked.'

'Okay. Sit tight. Wait for my call.'

'You got it.' Friesen hesitates. 'One more thing — he knows about the government bonds.'

A long, drawn-out pause from the other end. Then, 'Why on earth does he know about the bonds?'

'He nearly choked me out before we got off the plane. He's antsy, and I don't blame him. I had to give him something to keep him happy.'

There comes the unmistakable sound of Lars grinding his teeth. 'And is he happy now?'

'No. I can't string him along much longer.'

'Okay. Sit tight,' Lars repeats.

Friesen clicks off.

13

L ars hears the spook hang up and sets his jaw as he storms through the antechamber again.

This time, there's less hesitation.

He gives barely any thought to the power of Christian West, to the grave danger of making a mistake in the presence of "The Golden One." All he can focus on is the fact that King's going to put two and two together sooner rather than later, and then all bets are off.

He strides into the office with a certain urgency.

And finds himself staring down the barrel of a giant pistol.

Christian West still sits behind his grand desk, backlit by the glow of thousands of the D.C. skyline, but this time he leans forward with both elbows on the table, mostly to steady the aim of the Desert Eagle clutched in his right hand.

Lars knows the man has no combat experience to speak of, but with a gun that big, it doesn't much matter.

It's a straight shot, and it'll only take one of the .50 Action Express rounds to blow a fist-sized hole through

Lars' torso. He's not wearing body armour; he's in a creased suit, a size too big.

Game over.

'W-w-wha—?' he stammers.

West's eyes are glacial, unmoving. 'You didn't knock,' he says softly. There's a manic spark in his stare. He looks ready to pull the trigger, if only to see what'd happen. And he might. There's no reason not to send Lars Crawford straight to hell.

If the ship is going down, it's only fair — in fact, it's expected — that the captain goes down with it...

Lars stymies the intrusive thoughts and musters his courage. 'Can we cut the shit?'

West raises an eyebrow. Lars gets the strange sense that the man enjoys being spoken back to. At his level of the game, it must be a rare novelty.

He gestures with the massive pistol, like, *Go on.*

Lars holds up his phone. 'Word from South America. King's as fatigued as he's ever going to be. I know they plan to go higher in the morning, over twenty thousand feet, but he's not gonna get another altitude jump like that first one: zero to seventeen thousand. What I'm telling you is, his body's in survival mode, but it won't be for much longer.'

Still pointing the Desert Eagle at his chest, West cocks his head. 'Not much longer? You said it yourself — there's still more climbing to do, and the physical work at that altitude hasn't even begun. I want him at his very worst.'

'This will be his worst.' Lars stares at "The Golden One," refusing to wilt. 'You've never met Jason King, have you?'

'I've seen forty successful after-action reports. That tells me all I need to know.'

'*Most.* Not all,' Lars corrects, hoping he doesn't catch a .50 calibre bullet for his troubles. 'King adapts to disaster faster than anyone I've ever seen. Right now, his head's splitting, his guts are revolting, and he's probably as tired as he's ever been in his life. But the only reason that's going to keep him down is because he's not used to it. If he gets up tomorrow morning and feels the same, he'll just grit his teeth and soldier on like it's no problem. He might not feel a hundred percent, but he won't care. He'll do what he's supposed to do, whether he feels like it or not. And when he gets that way ... I've seen it too many times to count. It's like he beats his body into submission until it complies. His mind is iron. He'll hold the line as long as it takes to start feeling better. And, trust me, he'll start feeling better a hell of a lot faster than you think he will. I know what he's like.' He gazes over the top of West's head, searching for the right words. 'He's determination personified.'

He falls quiet to let "The Golden One" digest the spiel.

Eventually, West says, 'Is there more?'

'No, sir.'

The man rolls his eyes. 'Well, that was about the most motivational thing I've ever heard. What are you doing in this business? You should give self-help keynotes at conferences. "Win the morning, win the day," right?'

Lars lets the man mock. It's not like he has a choice. But he steels himself and says, 'I stand by what I said.'

Maybe no one does that when Christian West starts insulting them. Maybe they all wither before him. Because "The Golden One" seems genuinely impressed by Lars' steadfastness, and he gently lowers the Desert Eagle to the desk.

Lars masks a sigh of pure relief.

West rolls his tongue over his teeth, pupils flicking back and forth as he stares into the space between them.

Deep in thought.

Then, in one decisive motion, he leans forward, says, 'Okay,' and punches a number into one of the phones on the walnut.

Lars knows who he's calling: Argentina's Presidential Chief of Staff. Lars can't remember the man's name, but it doesn't much matter. The conversation is short and to the point; West puts it on speakerphone.

'Are your men inserted into Chile yet?' he asks in place of a greeting.

'Yes,' comes the accented reply. 'No problem there. They are bunkered down and preparing for—'

'They go first thing in the morning,' West orders. 'Move them through Copiapó for the clean-up, and then send them into the mountains.'

A momentary silence. 'Isn't that early?'

West's face flares in barely suppressed anger. 'Yes, it is.'

He waits for the protest, ready to pounce. But the Chief of Staff gets the message, reads West's tone, and replies with, 'First thing in the morning, then.' A pause. 'But won't your guy get it done before my men even enter the equation?'

'Probably,' West says. 'But I want every inch of that volcano covered in case he slips through my fingers. I don't expect him to, but you never know.' A quick glance at Lars. 'I'm told he's the best.'

The Chief of Staff says, 'My men are the best.'

Still locked in a staredown with Lars, West smiles. 'I'm counting on it, my friend.'

Lars takes the cue and hustles out of the office to make a call.

14

In a small shack on the outskirts of Copiapó, a satellite phone rings.

A huge man, six-four and built like a barrel, levers slowly off a mattress far too small for his two hundred and sixty pounds.

He's known only as Enzo.

Although he's headed an elite and secret unit of the *Agrupación de Fuerzas de Operaciones Especiales* — Argentina's Special Forces — for most of his adult life, very few of his grievous physical wounds can be attributed to his time in combat. The mottled scars running up his arms, his missing left ring finger, and the faded patch over his empty left eye socket are all gifts from his father, a brutal tyrant of a man who was an integral part of Operation Condor in South America during the 1970s.

His dad was trained to instil terror as quickly and efficiently as possible, and by all accounts the man was excellent at his job. He used to tell a preteen Enzo stories of peeling men's faces off, setting them on fire, cutting them open and pouring salt and bleach into their wounds. One time Enzo asked if all his victims were communists, and his father just laughed.

So Enzo has never known anything but senseless violence. He has only his father's tales as his clearest childhood memories.

Really, what hope did he have?

But he doesn't think about hope.

He thinks about doing his job, following in his dad's footsteps, despite how much he despises the old monster. For all the man's flaws, his father got shit done, clawed his way out of poverty in perhaps the messiest and bloodiest way possible. But he did it. Nothing changes the fact he was born in a *villa miseria* — what they call shanty towns in Argentina — and made it out. Very few do.

So if Enzo's psychopathy is genetic, and there's nothing he can do about the tendencies he inherited, he figures he might as well use them to get paid. No point letting them go to waste, mindlessly killing small animals or the homeless just to keep himself occupied.

Now he answers the phone and hears a voice say in Spanish, 'Change of plans. Go now. But make sure Copiapó's clear first.'

Enzo scratches at the bottom of his eyepatch. 'How clear?'

'You know.'

Enzo barely registers the order. By now, complying is as natural as breathing. If you've only got nine fingers and one eye, it usually rules you out of being a soldier, unless there are exceptional circumstances. Enzo used a little nepotism — his father was partly respected, mostly feared — and a hefty dose of natural talent to weasel his way into the Argentine Army, and he doesn't take it for granted that he managed to end up here: not just a member of an elite cadre of professionals, but the unit's *leader*.

There was probably an element of sympathy in the initial decision to accept him as a soldier. It only took one look at his face to see what his father had done to him in childhood.

Enzo doesn't care; he's here now, and his dad is in the ground. He put the old man there himself. Everybody knows it was him, but no one's ever mentioned it.

Not to his face, at least.

Now he says, 'Sure,' and snatches up his FN FAL battle rifle as he kills the call.

He collects his gear, gives the small shack the once-over, then steps outside into the bitter chill. Half his men are already outside the neighbouring huts, securing body armour and checking their weapons. Enzo can keep quiet when it's required, but out here it's not. They must have heard his two hundred and sixty pounds lumbering around and knew it was time to move. Plans and strategies mean nothing to them. Enzo's word is law, and if he says things have changed, that's the way it is.

One of his boys looks him up and down as the rest of them slip out of surrounding shacks. 'Should we bring the cars round?'

Enzo shakes his head. 'On foot through town. Nothing identifiable, hide your emblems. Make sure they see nothing, even if they see something. Understand?'

A sea of nods. By now all nine of his men are out of bed, geared up, and ready to roll in the grey light of dawn.

Enzo glances at his watch. 'Fifteen minutes, then we're ghosts.' He picks one of his troops at random and points a gloved finger. 'You. While you're in there, pick someone to kill. Make a statement.' He pans his finger across the chests of the other eight men. 'No one else. Injuries only. Broken bones, fine, but make it clean. Nothing permanent.' His gaze flicks over to Gabriel, the most reckless of the bunch, whose sadism gives Enzo's a run for its money. 'Understand?'

Gabriel nods again, followed quickly by everyone else.

'Beautiful,' Enzo says, adjusting his eyepatch against the wind. Then he shoos them away. '*Vamos.*'

They slink away, like ghosts floating into Copiapó.

15

E nzo hears the occasional scream as he walks down the arterial main road, but he knows there's far more silent suffering taking place in back-alleys and behind closed doors.

What escapes the odd victim's lips is just the tip of the iceberg.

His men are professional and do clean work. To any other unit, inflicting a citywide wave of terror in the span of fifteen minutes would be an impossible task, but he trains his boys day and night to carry out such requests. By now, Enzo trusts them. He used to have to hold their hands, walk them slowly through the process, show them exactly how to hurt someone to ensure they go tell everyone who will listen to keep their mouths shut and fall in line, but over the years the process has become second nature to his nine trained enforcers.

Now Enzo can keep his own hands clean, leave the serious stuff to the hungrier youths.

Maybe he's getting old and soft.

He hopes not.

He strolls past the university, its entrance building painted pink and set behind towering palm trees. Cowering silhouettes peer out from second-floor windows as he walks by. He's aware of two things: that there are eyes on him, and that no one will get brave. He's seen enough fear to know what it does to people, how it shrinks them into shells of themselves until they realise, deep down, that they're not who they thought they were.

We all believe we're heroes, he thinks, *until it's time to do what heroes do.*

He continues south-east, following the curve of the Copiapó River flowing behind the university, until the dust and dirt get thicker under his heavy boots and the urban sprawl gives way to the southernmost outskirts of the city. He's been walking for fourteen minutes and hasn't heard even the hint of a police siren. Already some of his men are flowing out of side streets and back onto the main avenue, several hundred feet behind him.

Still alone, he reaches a vast and empty field of dirt and saunters to a stop in front of its only attraction.

A shoddy taqueria truck.

A cardboard sign in the window advertises Peruvian food.

He gives the truck only a cursory glance and makes to move on, but a boy springs up into view with the speed of a carnival pop-up. Enzo notes a slight uptick in his own heart rate, and is quietly impressed with the child for giving him a fright. These days it's a novel experience.

'*¡Hola!*' the boy shouts. 'Do you also want *pan con chicharrón?*'

His Spanish is fast and furious, but the kid knows what he's saying.

'"Also"?' Enzo asks.

The child blinks. 'You are a soldier like the American. I thought you were together. Sorry. Do you want food? My mother is asleep but I can wake her up.'

Enzo looks slowly around. No witnesses on the street, very little passing traffic. Half his men are done in the city and are milling about at the edge of the field, waiting for the soldiers who haven't yet materialised to collect the SUVs and pick them up.

He turns back and sighs. 'No, boy. Don't wake your mother. What's your name?'

He doesn't know why he's asking. Maybe it's an attempt to give himself pause, but deep down he knows however much the kid humanises himself, it won't matter.

'David,' the boy says.

'David, I have a problem. My problem is that I'm not very hungry. But I'd like to give you some money. Would you be okay with that?'

David nods vigorously. His eyes are wide, and from that alone Enzo knows it's done.

But the child is energetic, curious, and unaware of etiquette. 'What's wrong with your eye?'

It's innocent enough. Enzo would expect nothing less from what looks to be an eight year old. But it would scare David if Enzo told the truth.

The truth is that his father held him down when he was fourteen years old and slashed his eyeball open, ended up pulling the whole thing from its socket as punishment for talking back. Blood sprayed everywhere and Enzo screamed and screamed and the old man just laughed and said, *'Learned your lesson, huh?'*

'An accident,' Enzo says softly. 'Now — the money. I have ten thousand pesos for you. Would you like that?'

David's eyes go wider, and he forgets about the eyepatch.

Enzo sees the kid running calculations. He can almost hear him think, *That's a lot of pan con chicharrón.*

He nods faster.

Enzo looks around conspiratorially and then nods to the field behind the truck. 'I'll meet you back there. If someone sees, they might try to steal the money from you.'

Even the possibility horrifies David, and he disappears from sight, making for the taqueira's back door. Enzo circles around the truck and meets the boy on a small, dry patch of land that serves as their rear yard. David beams as Enzo walks up to him and makes to shout something excitedly.

Enzo touches a finger to his lips. *Quiet.*

David's hands fall by his side and he keeps his mouth shut. Enzo kneels in front of him, and still has to hunch so they can see eye-to-eye. The child is a tiny, fragile twig, a direct contrast to the six-four brute.

Enzo glances left to look through the swinging rear door, which hasn't fully shut yet, and sees through to a sliver of the tiny bedroom up the back of the truck. A large woman slumps on a bare mattress, facing the wall, breathing slowly and deeply.

Dead to the world.

Enzo looks back at David and leans in close, his voice a whisper. 'You are so young. This isn't your fault. Kids just can't stay quiet.'

Like a leaping panther, he clamps his hands around David's small throat and squeezes so hard that the child doesn't have a hope in hell of crying out. Only feet from his mother, he thrashes and kicks and his eyes practically bug out of his skull as his face turns purple. He doesn't even manage to wheeze.

Enzo is unbelievably strong, and, mercifully, the boy is dead in ten seconds.

The soldier lowers the body to the dust.

But one skinny arm unspools and slaps the ground, and it makes a small *thud*. The truck groans as the heavy woman sits bolt upright within. She faces the wall still, clearing her eyes, then her gaze swings over to the rear door.

Enzo charges inside, a brick wall of bodyweight. He falls straight onto her with savage ferocity. He seizes her by the neck, pins her to the mattress, and proceeds to squeeze the life out of her, too.

By the time he's done, he's panting for breath.

She should consider herself lucky. He hates expending needless energy, but if he went any slower she'd have seen her son's corpse.

This way, she didn't even get a glimpse.

Maybe, he thinks as he looks down at her bloodshot, unseeing eyes, *there's* some *humanity left in me.*

Catching his breath, he staggers out of the truck and heads back out onto the road. The SUVs are waiting, stripped of their licence plates and full of his men. He beelines for one of the vehicles and says, '*Vamos,*' as he leaps inside.

By the time they're out of Copiapó, he's already forgotten about the taqueria.

16

'U*p!'*
Friesen's voice cuts through the wind and washes over King's tent like a blaring alarm.

King sits up, grimaces at the presence of a drilling headache, then forcibly wipes the expression off his face. He still feels like shit. He barely slept, had to stagger out of his tent at three in the morning to finally throw up everything in his stomach, and every time he moves a muscle, his heart starts to race at the energy required. But none of that matters anymore. He's here to do a job and it's critically important that he does it well.

And besides, he thinks, *everyone else is going through the same thing.*

But when he clambers out of his tent, Friesen looks fine. The man stands fully upright in his cold-weather gear, hands in pockets, watching King and Evans drag themselves out of their respective bedchambers. King looks over at the climber and sees that Evans looks much better than he did last night. So it's just him on a solo journey through hell.

Doesn't matter, he reminds himself again.

They eat a quick breakfast that one of the drivers prepares as the sun rises brilliantly over the mountains. King forces down some meagre calories as he stares slack-jawed at the scenery. Nothing he's seen before is comparable. They're above the clouds, and the shadows cast by some of the severe peaks around them are the size of small cities.

Then he looks over his shoulder and sees Ojos del Salado for the first time. 'Holy shit.'

Invisible in the darkness the night before, the golden sun reveals the volcano in all its glory. It's impossibly huge, like a monument erected by the gods. Coupled with the terrain that surrounds it, King can't help feeling awestruck. But as he focuses on the massive slope beneath the upper reaches of the volcano, he can't do anything about the creeping anxiety, either.

'Doesn't look like there's much of a trail,' he says, glancing at the jeeps like it might be revealed that they can fly.

'There isn't,' Evans says. 'Some serious off-roading coming up.'

King feels queasy enough without bouncing around in a jeep pitched at a forty-five degree angle. What's more concerning is how little he knows about their plan once they *reach* the altitude they're gunning for.

'And when we get above twenty thousand feet,' he says, looking at Friesen, 'what then?'

The spook just raises his eyebrows, as if it's a mystery to him, too.

'You'll see,' the man grunts, and turns away.

King looks at Evans, who shrugs. It's not like the climber has any answers. He probably doesn't even know why he's here, kept in the dark the same as King. Gunning up the tallest volcano in the world in a modified jeep doesn't exactly require Evans' talents. There's no complicated mountaineering here; King has yet to see a rope, a harness, or a carabiner. Even if there was proper climbing involved, he's confident he could handle it himself. A decent chunk of his black-ops missions have taken place in inhospitable terrain.

So the presence of Reece Evans is almost as much of a mystery as Allan Friesen.

King stops thinking, because in most cases thinking achieves nothing. He just assembles his gear, hauls it back into the jeep, slides across the rear seats, and steels himself.

It ends up being worse than anything he could have braced for.

Just as his body was beginning to adjust to seventeen thousand feet, slowly figuring out how to deal with the frightening lack of oxygen in the air, they set off for higher ground. Half an hour into the drive, King's watch displays only eight hundred feet of elevation gain since they left the Atacama Refuge.

But by this point, the moment you go higher, everything gets exponentially worse.

The headache comes screaming back, the energy demands on his body are massive and unrelenting, and thirty-three minutes after leaving the refuge, he leans out the window and vomits his breakfast onto the jagged rocks. He slumps back into the seat, fighting shivers. The wind smashes him. Already his lips are raw.

The next hour moves like molasses.

The whole time, King fights his mind.

Tries to empty it.

He figures this is why he's here.

Finally the convoy rattles to a halt on a stretch of flat ground, a miniature plateau slapped on one side of the volcano's upper reaches. What appears to be the summit looms above, and King points up to it as his empty guts cramp. 'We're not going a little further?'

'No,' Friesen says. 'Here's good.'

The big man is pale and looks woozy.

About time, King thinks.

Strangely enough, Evans now looks okay as he gets out of the other jeep. There's some colour in his face and some energy in his eyes. The climber glances at Friesen and smirks, grateful that he and the spook have seemingly switched places. Clearly, ascending so rapidly from zero to seventeen thousand feet threw him off, but if the guy's spent considerable time tackling the tallest peaks in the world, his body must know how to adapt. He's handling it well.

King understands why Evans is here now.

There's nothing up here the man hasn't seen before.

The drivers take oxygen when needed as they set up a small camp on the flat ground, but it's not helping them much anymore. They look like walking corpses. At least after they get the tents up, their work is largely done. As they erect the tents, King stands beside Evans and takes in the new view.

It's unbelievable.

'Tres Cruces,' Evans says, pointing to a distant summit. He moves his finger. 'And that's Pissis. Mate, isn't it beautiful?'

It might be, but King can't focus.

He's fighting bodily sensations he's never felt before.

And he thought he'd experienced everything.

Evans notes the lack of response, turns, and grabs King by the shoulders. He studies his face. King stands there, trying not to retch.

'Mate,' Evans says, 'incredible stuff. Zero to six and a half thousand metres in less than twenty four hours. You're a machine. Keep your head screwed on and don't panic. You're fit enough, you'll adjust.' A pause. 'Or you'll spiral into full-blown altitude sickness. Either way, it's out of your hands, so *hakuna matata.*'

King manages a smile at the Lion King reference.

Then Friesen shouts, 'Get over here! Time for hill sprints!'

King feels genuine fear in the pit of his stomach, and suddenly he sees why they flew him all the way here for this.

You can't simulate this sort of torture.

He drags himself over to the spook.

17

King's goal in training camps is always to shock his instructors.

No matter what's asked of him, he throws himself into his present task like a man possessed. He doesn't think about the accumulated fatigue, or his injuries and ailments, or any self-doubt that might worm its way into his mind. He just does what he's told like a robot programmed to exert effort: all action, no thought.

Eventually his instructors realise nothing they do can faze him, and it demoralises them.

They get dejected.

They end up easing off the gas, because the more pressure they heap on King's shoulders, the more he seems to enjoy it. It screws with their heads, trying to break someone who no longer cares about self-preservation.

Here, on the upper reaches of Ojos del Salado, it doesn't quite go that way.

Friesen points at an incline of frozen dirt and says, 'Up. As fast as you can.'

King allows himself a moment of weakness. Despite

what many of his superiors think, he's not superhuman. Every day he feels everything they believe he's immune to: doubt, anxiety, stress — all in enormous doses. Now he bends over and puts his hands on his knees, and he can feel Friesen thinking, *I knew he wasn't special.*

King stares at the rocks beneath his feet, composing himself.

Breathe in.

Hold.

Release.

Go.

He straightens up and charges up the slope like a berserker.

Friesen didn't tell him how far to climb, so he forgets about external goals and just focuses on pushing himself, clawing for more progress.

Always *more.*

He slips half a dozen times on patches of ice, but pushes himself back up over and over again until his palms are scraped and bloodied. He only manages twenty seconds of upward momentum before the exhaustion hits him like a freight train.

He sits down involuntarily on a rock jutting out from the slope, gasping for breath like he's drowning.

Physiologically, he is.

At twenty thousand feet, there's less than ten percent oxygen in the air. It's like someone's told him to sprint for his life while holding a cloth over his mouth and nose. The discomfort is indescribable. His brain screams at him to curl into a ball and cry.

Instead he stands up, sucking in air with ragged breaths, and lumbers back down to Friesen.

The soldier looks him up and down. His face betrays nothing. 'Again.'

The words almost explode from King's lips: *I can't.*

He catches them before they slip out.

Doesn't let his doubt show.

He keeps his face expressionless and starts back up the hill, albeit slower. A slow jog is enough to convince his brain he's on the verge of death. Strangely enough, there's no muscle soreness, no lactic acid to make his legs heavy and swollen, because down at sea level it would be a cakewalk to run twice up a hill. What's killing him — literally and figuratively — is the sheer effort required when deep breaths provide no fuel. Physically unable to recover, it feels like he's being held underwater with a two hundred pound weight on his chest, fighting to get his nostrils above the surface.

He gasps and pants, but it achieves nothing.

He makes it to the same rock and staggers back down, throat already raw.

When he reaches Friesen again, he's in bad shape. Two minutes of activity and he's effectively crippled, hurting in so many ways that it's hard to separate each sensation.

Just a tsunami of pain.

'How ... long ... are we ... here?' he splutters between breaths.

Friesen regards him coldly. 'As long as I say.'

'I meant ... at this ... altitude. How ... long ... is the camp?'

'I answered that. As long as I say. Now, up the hill again.'

The splitting headache almost makes King take a knee. He realises he has to be honest. 'I ... can't run.'

'I didn't say how fast. This isn't about speed. You understand?'

King understands. He wishes he didn't. Early in his

career, Lars Crawford brought him a scientific research
paper with the definition: *'Endurance is the struggle to
continue against a mounting desire to stop.'*

He's never forgotten those words.

He makes it up and down the slope twice more, battling
the sensation that his boots are moving through thick mud.
After four total climbs, he can barely walk. He drags his legs
behind him, and when he gets back down to Friesen he tries
to stay standing, but he can't. He slumps on his rear on the
frozen ground, breath steaming in front of his face. He
retches, hugs his knees to his chest, and tries valiantly to
recover.

Reece Evans walks over and sits down beside him. The
climber faces forward, and although he speaks softly, King
hears every word.

'I think I understand why I'm here now,' he says.

18

Between breaths, King manages to mumble, 'Yeah?'

Evans ruminates for a moment. 'I summited K2 last year. Most people don't know it, but it's a harder mountain than Everest. I used everything to get to the top and left myself nothing for the journey down. I was on death's door — I collapsed in the snow. Two climbers I'd been descending with left me for dead. I don't blame them — up there, that's the game. They barely had the energy to carry themselves out, let alone my useless weight. And if they'd tried, we'd have been three frozen corpses on the mountain. It was either me or all of us. But after they left, I must have tapped into something deeper. Ain't much of it I remember, but I picked myself up and kept going on empty. Somehow I made it down. I think maybe your bosses heard about that, mate.'

'Probably,' King admits. 'I could use some advice in that department.'

He's not exaggerating. His gas tank is *below* empty. He couldn't imagine forcing himself onward.

He figures Friesen could just leave him for dead here, if that's what the spook wanted.

Evans finally looks at him. 'Here's what I did, lad...' His eyes go cloudy as he connects dots for the first time. 'Y'know, maybe it's not so different after all ... what you and I do. When I first met you, I thought you were another species. But up there, above eight thousand metres, alone in the death zone ... it's all a head game, mate. It's you and your thoughts and that's it. Same as when I'm sure you've found yourself in deep shit behind enemy lines, thoughts spiralling, fighting off panic...'

'All of life is a head game,' King says simply. 'I see that, and so do you, because we voluntarily put ourselves in the worst situations imaginable. That's all it is.'

'Yeah,' Evans agrees. 'It's pretty powerful shit, hey?'

King shrugs. He's indescribably tired...

Evans watches him closely, then seems to remember what he first walked over to talk about.

'If I had a gun to your head,' the climber says, 'and I told you to take a single step further, would you do it?'

King gazes at the view. The question seems rhetorical, but Evans expects an answer.

'No shit,' he says.

'Does it matter if the gun is real?' Evans asks.

'What?'

'What if you just imagined it was there?'

'If it wasn't there, I wouldn't be in danger.'

'What difference does it make? You said you'd be able to keep going if I had a gun to your head. So why can't you just pretend it is? Nothing physically changes.'

A pause. 'Oh.'

'You *can* take a step. You're choosing not to. I wouldn't be dragging you by the collar, would I?'

'No.'

'Do you understand?'

Something strange rolls over King; a beautiful hint of knowledge, no more than a passing flash. 'I think I do. Almost...'

'When the choice is life or death, it's so obvious. You just take another step. You don't think about how easy or hard it is. The alternative is a bullet through the skull, so you do it.'

King says nothing.

'The gun isn't real,' Evans says, 'even if it is. Do you understand?'

Again, 'Almost.'

'There's always more to give, mate. You've put your life on the line a hundred times already and you still can't see it.'

King keeps staring out over the mountain range. 'No, I see.'

It hurts like hell, but he picks himself up and trudges slowly back up the slope. He treats each step like someone's holding everyone he ever loved hostage, and will kill them all if he doesn't plant his foot six inches further forward.

It works.

He makes it up and back a fifth time, albeit at a snail's pace.

Friesen watches the resurgence unfold. When King lumbers back down to face the spook, he staggers to a halt and sways, but doesn't collapse. Somehow he stays on his feet.

Friesen nods, impressed. 'Okay. That's good. You get an hour off your feet while I set up what's next.'

'And what *is* ... next?' King mumbles.

'Clandestine insertion and extraction procedures. You know them, but I want you practicing them in a state of survival.'

King limps to his tent and collapses into it.

He lies there for maybe twenty seconds, semi-conscious, until the world falls away.

19

Reece Evans' beautiful philosophy ends up being no help at all.

King wakes from an hour's nap feeling twice as exhausted as when he went to sleep.

When he rolls from his back to his side, his heart rate skyrockets, beating twice a second even though he's still stretched out on top of his sleeping bag. He feels the rapid thud of his pulse in his throat and takes a deliberately slow breath that does very little to calm him down.

As he sits up, he realises he's screwed.

His muscles are lead, his bones impossibly dense. Each tiny movement takes all the energy he can muster and brings with it a stab of anxiety, because even when he's been grievously injured on covert operations, he's never felt like this — not once in his life.

It's the most tired he's ever been.

He can will himself to take "one more step" as much as he wants: it doesn't change the fact that he's an hour and a half into this training camp and already has nothing left. He thinks back to when Friesen suggested he could last seven days. He'd laugh at the prediction if he could muster the energy.

That's when the paranoid thoughts start creeping in. Exhaustion and negativity go hand in hand. He sits there, arms wrapped around his knees, rocking back and forth as if the rhythm will generate motivation that doesn't exist, and he wonders why he's really here. He doesn't buy Friesen's explanation anymore. If they wanted to push him to his limits, they could easily do that at sea level and reap far more benefit than grinding him into paste within sixty minutes of arriving at a spot thousands of miles from home.

They want you depleted to zero, his darkest thoughts tell him. *They want you defenceless.*

It terrifies him because if it's true, then they've already succeeded, and there's not a damn thing he can do to change it. Even if he lies in his tent another few hours, he won't recover. At sea level, it'd be a different story, but aside from gunning it down the side of the volcano in one of the jeeps until he tastes oxygen-rich air, it's going to be impossible to shake this fatigue.

He tipped himself way over the edge on that fifth hill climb, probably for no reason at all.

He scolds himself for his idiocy.

No more, he decides. Whatever Friesen's setting up, he won't take part, not until he's spoken directly to Lars Crawford and received some kind of clarification on precisely what he's doing here.

Every inch of movement laboured, he unzips his tent and yanks the North Face polyester aside to reveal the surrounding camp.

He takes one look out the door and his stomach sinks.

I fucking knew it, he thinks as he uses what little energy he has left to snatch up his SIG Sauer.

There's a single human target he can put squarely in his sights, but he doesn't bother, because he knows Reece Evans means no harm. The climber is completely unaware that he's being observed. Evans sits in a deep squat beside one of the jeeps, his ass resting on his heels, sporting the sort of effortless flexibility and strength that those in the modern world have lost. One hand is planted on the jeep's body, and the other tugs at his own hair, his face twisted in a grimace as he stares at the wheels.

All four tyres are flat.

From the way the metal wheels press directly into the ground, every morsel of air sucked from the inner tubes, King knows someone took a knife to the rubber.

Knows it's sabotage.

With Evans none the wiser, King takes a peek around the edge of the tent door and sees his worst nightmare come to life.

The second jeep sits a few dozen feet away, identical to the first: all the tyres shredded.

Equally useless.

Everything gets real. Already it's a guaranteed multi-day trek down to a reasonable altitude, and that's not even taking into consideration the fact that there's no sign of the drivers, no sign of Allan Friesen.

Fighting off a wave of fear, King reaches for his pack and busies himself with the piece of equipment he appropriated from the pallet on the plane the day before.

When he's done, he struggles out of his tent and pans the SIG across the upper reaches of Ojos del Salado.

Nothing.

No snipers aiming down at him, no sight of Friesen behind a rifle. Nothing he can see, at least, and judging by the fact that his skull remains intact, he doubts he's missing anything. But sweeping the terrain with his sidearm brings serious issues to light: namely, that just raising his arms makes him pant for breath.

He lowers the weapon and turns toward the jeeps.

Evans looks badly rattled, and he stares unblinking at King, still squatting by one of the tyres.

'Mate, tell me this is some twisted training exercise,' he says, unable to keep the tremor from his voice. 'Tell me I'm out of the loop. Otherwise...'

He doesn't need to finish. The silence speaks for itself.

Otherwise we're both dead. No ifs, ands, or buts.

A panicking Reece Evans only makes King feel more helpless. Before this, the climber was stoic and unflappable, and now there's cracks in his exterior. His blue eyes twitch, and the rugged lines etched into his forehead are deeper as he wears a frown for the first time since King met him.

King crosses the campsite, holding the gun low. 'You see where everyone went?'

'I was in my tent for twenty minutes,' Evans says as King approaches. 'I came back out to this shit.' A strange look comes over his face. 'Are you...?'

'What?'

He scratches his jaw, face creased with worry. 'Are you unpopular?'

King looks Evans up and down for any hint that the climber might turn on him out of fear and desperation. His gaze lingers a moment on the man's boots, then he wobbles on the spot and sits down in a flustered heap on the freezing ground.

'Shit,' he mumbles, and the SIG spills from his hand, landing between his feet. He picks the gun back up with shaky fingers, but he's only got a half-hearted grip on the barrel itself, and his eyes begin drooping closed.

'Fuck, mate,' Evans says, inching closer to him. 'Looks like full-blown altitude sickness.'

'Mmm,' King mumbles, eyelashes now touching as his lids drift further shut.

'Here, lemme help you up. Gotta get you out of—'

Evans was moving his right arm surreptitiously at first, but mid-sentence he swings it like a whip and brings the solid KA-BAR knife out from behind his back.

He plunges it dead centre into King's chest.

20

Instead of feeling seven inches of USMC-approved steel split his sternum and plunge into his heart, King only feels a blunt impact.

It still smashes the breath out of him.

Evans is deceptively strong, all lean sinew, his frame tough as rawhide.

But King just looks up at the climber — his eyes now fully open — as the KA-BAR skewers uselessly into the Kevlar vest he took from one of the pallets and slipped on under his jacket before he left the tent.

Evans stumbles back a half-step, his arm deadened by the shuddering impact. His whole body rattled after he put everything he had into the swing and hit the equivalent of a brick wall. His wrist is likely broken, and the knife falls from his hand as he plants his feet to steady himself. He sure didn't pretend to drop it, not like how King faked losing his grip on the SIG.

King's tired, but not *that* tired.

King rears to his feet, snatching the knife off the ground on his way up, then seizes Evans by the throat before the man can understand how screwed he is. King's exhausted to the bone, but he's still got unnatural raw power, which would hinder him if he wanted to summit an eight-thousand metre peak but helps him now to just toss Evans off his feet like a rag doll.

The climber sprawls on the ground, lashes his skull on a sharp rock, and blood sprays from a long cut down one side of his temple as he scrambles for purchase. King looms over him, kicks him in the ribs hard enough to shatter two or three of them, then grabs him by the collar and slams him back against one side of the jeep, accompanied by a hollow *boom*.

Already, Evans' face is a crimson mask.

It's only going to get worse.

King isn't sure of the exact science, but he knows it's harder to stop bleeding at altitude — something to do with blood pressure. Evans' cut is pouring like a faucet, and already he's blinded.

'Mate,' the man gasps, droplets flying from his lips, eyes squeezed painfully shut. 'Mate, please, I'm ... oh, fuck...'

King can't waste his energy on needless anger — he has frighteningly little stamina left. Besides, what would anger change?

His voice robotic and expressionless, he pins Evans harder to the jeep and says, 'Start talking.'

'I'm talking,' the climber pants. 'Don't you hear me? Look, there's...' He trails off, unsure what to say or how to say it.

'You've got three seconds, Reece.'

'Listen...'

'I'm listening,' King says. 'One second.'

Being rendered blind at such a crucial moment is driving Evans mad. He blinks hard, trying to clear the blood with his eyelashes, but he only winces and groans as the crimson flow seeps deeper beneath his eyelids. His world must be stinging, burning frustration, along with the fire in his ribs. King's sure he heard a couple of bones snap after the kick to the mid-section.

The allotted second passes, and now they're in overtime.

King's in no mood for delays.

He has no intel, no situational awareness, and detests being out in the open like this with no idea where the other players are. He knows nothing about either of the drivers, and Friesen could be anywhere, doing anything.

'Time's up,' King says.

He means it.

Evans is thinking hard, his other senses heightened by his loss of vision, and his mouth seals in a hard line as he comes to some sort of mental resolution. Before he was shaking, crazed with fear from a dose of pure adrenaline, but now he straightens up and steels himself. He stops resisting.

'I'm not gonna talk,' he says. 'Just kill me. It's done. You won, I lost. Let's not pretend it's gonna be anything else, mate.'

King shrugs for no one to see. It's frustrating not to get context, but he won't lose sleep over it. Making it out of this alive is his number one priority.

Evans senses this is the end, and he must feel a final stab of curiosity, because he asks softly, 'How did you know?'

King holds him at arm's length. 'You had a drop of blood on your left boot.'

'But you were already wearing the vest.'

'I didn't trust anyone. Then I saw the blood, knew for sure I didn't trust *you*, and faked the wooziness.'

Evans swallows some of his own blood, coughs, and

sighs. 'Fair play. I really thought that'd work. Shows what the fuck I know...'

'Last chance to talk.'

'Don't patronise me. Well done, mate. Take your win.'

To the very end, Reece Evans is no-nonsense. He knows King is a professional, isn't going to drag this out any more than he needs to. If you get too deep into the morality of it all, you lose your edge. Avoiding hesitation is the answer to most of the major difficulties in the field.

So King brings the KA-BAR knife up and slams the blade deep into the left side of the climber's chest.

Skewers his heart, the way Evans tried to do to him.

21

E vans isn't wearing a vest.

Eyes still forced shut involuntarily, the climber gasps, snarls, and fades. It takes less than a second from the time the blade splits the skin for the life to ebb from his face. King's killed a few men in the same fashion, and all the ones who came before lasted longer than Evans; they held on to consciousness for dear life, knowing it was their last moments on earth.

Evans had already accepted his fate.

Spending a decent chunk of your life at the mercy of nature must humble you.

In some strange way, King respects the man. At least Evans didn't apologise. He was who he was, he did what he did, and nothing he could say would change his fate, so he didn't bother.

You won, I lost.

Such simple words, but they carry tremendous weight now that Evans is a corpse. King imagines that in the climber's final moments, he pictured himself slumped in the snow below the summit of K2, seeing a version of events where he never made it back to his feet, never continued down the mountain.

A peaceful death.

He went to the grave more graceful than most.

King leaves the KA-BAR embedded up to the hilt in Evans' chest as he lets go of the body and watches it crumple in an unceremonious heap beside the jeep. He has a similar knife in his tent, and he doesn't need Evans' — he has a SIG: far more effective. At first, he suspected everything that left Evans' lips to be a lie, but if the climber resorted to trying to stab King to death, he was certainly being truthful about his lack of combat experience.

King crouches by the vehicle and sweeps the SIG's barrel across the upper reaches of the volcano again.

Nothing.

Same as before.

Only wind and desolation.

On a hunch, he rises and crosses to the western edge of the small plain where they established their camp. He wastes no movement, and doesn't let his guard down for a millisecond. He can't afford it. He's aided by a hefty boost in energy, but it troubles him that he feels okay. He knows it's temporary and artificial, cortisol flooding his bloodstream, stress chemicals pumping him up in the interest of self-preservation. Eventually he'll crash, and the thought terrifies him — an adrenaline dump at this altitude ... he couldn't imagine the exhaustion.

He reaches a low wall formed naturally by a series of jagged rocks, masking a shallow ditch from view of the tents behind him. He spotted the divot in the terrain when they first rolled into camp, and knows on the other side, the volcano slope plummets dramatically downward. He can't escape this way, but he doesn't want to.

He takes a look into the ditch and sees exactly what he expects to see.

The drivers are dead.

They lie one on top of the other in the shape of an "X." Both bodies stare lifelessly up at the sky, their throats slashed. The wounds are crude and messy; Evans favoured brute force over any real skill or precision. It confirms what King already suspected: Evans really *was* a climber, wasn't one of Friesen's colleagues feigning ignorance.

Which makes it more impressive that he actually got the job done while King was passed out in his tent.

And it's all the more confusing that Friesen didn't do it.

Where are you, Allan? King thinks, looking from driver to driver as if one of them might sit up and answer him. After only a moment he tears his gaze away; there's nothing for him here.

He forms a barebones plan. *Stock up on MREs and water, hike downhill for a few hours, clear your head, figure it out from there.*

He doesn't need more detail than that. Every second he spends above twenty thousand feet is draining his energy, squeezing him like a sponge, and the old General Patton quote rings true: 'A good plan, violently executed now, is better than a perfect plan next week.'

He strides to the edge of the plain and stares down the never-ending edifice of Ojos del Salado, searching for the route the jeeps used to get up here in the first place. He figures retracing their off-roading is his best chance of avoiding sheer drops or impassable terrain. He only manages a half-second glimpse directly downhill before he sees something in his peripheral vision and throws himself down out of sight.

Panic mode.

He suppresses the terror as he processes what he saw. He's certain they were silhouettes, way down below, dotted across the length of the edifice. He definitely registered tiny flickers of movement amidst the scenery. And there was a pattern to the unconnected shapes, as if an invisible rope tied them all together. He knows what that means because the very same training is drilled into *him*: they were a squad, a unit of combatants.

So it's far worse than he thought.

Lying prone at the edge of the plain, he doesn't dare take another peek. There has to be nearly a dozen men coming for him, given just how much movement he spotted across the landscape. Which, he realises, begs the question: *Why bother with someone like Reece Evans?*

He knows the answer. Whoever's doing this, they underestimated him. They figured altitude would strip away all his advantages and amplify Evans' abilities. *Find the guy who handles thin air the best and put a weapon in his hands.*

The soldiers moving up the volcano will be better trained, but worse without oxygen.

King stays hunched out of sight as he rises slowly to one knee.

Then he turns to run for his gear, planning to properly equip himself.

He doesn't get the chance.

Allan Friesen snuck up behind him, and when King pivots, the spook sticks a gun in his face.

22

King absorbs it all in a flash.

That's it, he thinks. *I'm dead.*

He holds his SIG at a forty-five degree angle, but the slightest twitch of movement and Friesen will blow him away. He could shove a finger in the trigger guard and pull, maybe hit Friesen in the stomach, but it would guarantee his own demise.

So he freezes up and hopes for mercy.

It's a bad plan.

But Friesen lowers his gun. The man's eyes are wide. 'What the fuck are you doing?!'

King hesitates. 'You're not...?'

'I'm not *what*?' Friesen hisses, unable to believe his eyes. He glances back at Evans' body, flabbergasted. Then he turns back. 'You gonna explain that?'

When Evans stabbed King in the chest, he tore a slit straight through the layers of Gore-Tex before the blade met the Kevlar. In the form of an explanation, King sticks his fingers in the slit and tears hard, revealing the bulletproof vest underneath. The point of impact is clear, showing where Evans slammed the knife home and scratched up the vest.

'He tried to skewer me,' King says. 'The drivers weren't as lucky.'

Friesen's eyes widen further. He looks back at Evans again, as if seeing the climber in a new light. But as hard as he tries, he can't seem to imagine it. He faces King for a second time. 'You're full of shit.'

King doesn't care what Friesen thinks.

He's just surprised to be alive.

'Just then,' King says, 'why didn't you shoot?'

Friesen stares. 'What are you *talking* about?'

The spook is reeling, still processing the fact that three of their party are dead and both vehicles are sabotaged.

'You really didn't know, huh?' King says, more to himself than Friesen. He points at Evans' body. 'Had you met him before all this?'

Friesen shakes his head. Rapid calculations are taking place behind the spook's eyes. Above all else, he's adaptable. It dawns on him exactly what's taken place and he says, 'Where are the drivers?'

'In that ditch.'

Friesen's gaze pans from the ditch to the jeeps and their shredded tyres. 'Well, looks like we're hiking out.'

King shakes his head. 'There are men headed up here. Ten or so.'

Friesen pauses, expressionless. Hearing news like that, anyone else would descend into full-blown panic, but Friesen is with the Special Activities Center and his specialty, it seems, is keeping a cool head in the face of certain doom.

'How far out?' he asks.

'Couple miles at least. I only saw dots in the landscape.

We've got some time.' King regards him coldly. 'Did you know about this?'

'Does it *look* like I knew about this?'

'I don't know. You sure kept your cards close to your chest before this. If you were acting then, you could be acting now.'

At first Friesen seems hesitant, then he realises there's no point being secretive anymore.

'Because I didn't trust Reece,' he admits, 'and I didn't trust you. On the plane I took his phone from his bag — neither of you saw, you were both zoned out. I broke the passcode and found a private email inbox he'd tried to encrypt. I got in. He's not quite CIA-calibre. I learned two things: he's a gambler in deep with loan sharks, and he made contact with someone in Argentina who I believe has a direct line to those in power.'

King absorbs the revelations. 'Some plot from our side? Above the both of us?'

Friesen shakes his head. 'My working theory was that Evans was going to sell us out to pay off his gambling loans. There must be some members of government who don't know about the hundreds of millions in bonds that we bought. All they see is their bosses giving us free rein to traipse around on Ojos del Salado unsupervised — they don't know why we're being allowed, and it drives them mad. Either they reached out to Reece, or he reached out to them. Either way, they're happy, even if Reece ended up getting himself killed. He gave them our location and they're sending in their best to finish it. I think they plan to leave our bodies here. That way, the U.S. has no choice but to publicly admit guilt on the international stage. "*Yes, we have a clandestine program of killers operating outside of the rules, and, yes, we were running around in South America, armed to*

the teeth, and trying to blackmail their leaders into compliance."
It's a bad look.'

'But then your mystery boss comes calling for the hundreds of millions he's owed. That's the whole point of the blackmail.'

'These people don't know, or if they do, they don't care.'

King tries to think it all through, but it's hard to concentrate on anything other than the fact that trained killers are ghosting up the volcano towards them and he's perhaps the most physically spent he's ever been.

He looks sceptically at Friesen. 'You suspected all this, and you didn't pull the pin? You didn't alert anyone?'

'I was trying to work out where your allegiance lay. I thought you might be bought, too. Now you've cleared that up for me.'

King stares. 'I don't believe any of that. Not a word.'

'Okay,' Friesen replies.

Which asks the silent question: *What are you going to do about it?* King imagines the rest of what Friesen's thinking. *Argentine troops are coming for our heads, and I'm all you've got. It doesn't matter what you believe or don't believe.*

And he's right.

So King puts his doubt aside and just asks, 'You won't backstab me like Reece?'

No guarantee he'll get a truthful answer, but he's close to collapse and needs an ally, needs some small reassurance.

Friesen looks at King's chest. 'Reece *front*stabbed you. And if I wanted you dead, you'd be dead. You know that.'

'That's a fair point.' King glances over his shoulder at the ridge. 'Any ideas?'

Friesen half-smirks. 'I smelled a rat long before I took Reece's phone. Even when they sent me to location scout, I knew something was up. So I put a failsafe in place, the first time I came up here. Just in case.'

Puzzle pieces connect in King's head. 'You were up here longer than a single day, weren't you?'

'Of course,' Friesen finally admits. 'That's why I'm acclimatised. You were onto me from the jump.'

He points at King and taps the side of his head — *You're smart* — then turns and jogs for the ditch that the drivers lie dead in. He leapfrogs the rock wall, traverses the ditch and scrabbles down the slope on the far side: the one King considered lethal.

There must be a rock shelter down there, a shallow cave at the base of the steep slope, because moments after Friesen disappears from sight, King hears an engine fire to life.

As soon as he registers the noise, he breaks into a sprint.

Any sort of physical activity is hell, given the condition of his body, but he's already forgotten what it's like to feel normal.

Constant suffering is his new baseline.

He sprints to collect his duffel from his tent, then runs across the plain while slinging it over his back and tightening the shoulder straps. He leaps down into the ditch, scrambles over the opposite lip, and slides uncontrollably down the slope. It's almost a free fall. For a moment he thinks he's botched it, and fears there's nothing to prevent him gaining momentum and continuing down the side of the volcano like a spinning top, breaking every bone in his body and pulverising his brain to mush...

...but his boots slam into a large rock sticking out from the dirt and he collects himself in an ungainly heap on the hillside.

Now the sound of the engine is a dull roar in his ears, overpowering the rasping and scratching of his own laboured breathing. He looks across the slope and sees exactly what he predicted: a crepuscular cave underneath the plain above, as if a giant deity scooped solid rock out of the hillside thousands of years before. Twin headlights flare in the relative gloom, identical to those of the two useless vehicles up above.

All King can think looking at the jeep is, *How the fuck did you get it in there?*

There are time for questions later.

He scrambles horizontally across the slope, stomach lurching every time he looks down, picking his way from handhold to handhold. At one point he snatches a small rock and it tears away from the mountainside, taking a tiny avalanche of dirt with it. In his haste to grab a backup handhold, he makes too frantic of a movement, and his feet slip on the rocks below. With desperation, he lunges sideways and secures a new perch, but the near-death experience comes with a burst of adrenaline and he knows there's next to nothing left in his system.

His throat is shredded raw from breathing so hard as he heaves himself up into the rock shelter and rounds to the jeep's passenger side.

He throws the door open and effectively collapses in the seat, tossing his duffel in the back.

Behind the wheel, Friesen takes one look at him and says, 'Do you have the energy to hold on?'

'No,' King mumbles.

'Well, you're really gonna have to.'

'How did you—?'

'Get the jeep up here?'

King nods. *You read my mind.*

Friesen winces as he answers, probably remembering how gnarly it was. 'There was a way up. It's incredibly fucking sketchy, but I got it done. Nearly flipped the whole thing twice — hood over trunk. Steepest thing I've ever tackled. But I was just imagining being double-crossed here, and after that there was no way I was bailing. I had a hunch I'd need it. I was right.'

'I believe you about suspecting a double-cross,' King says. 'Everything else is bullshit. You didn't take Reece's phone. He's not some gambler who sold us out.'

Friesen looks over and, in one of the strangest experiences of King's life, just grins at him. 'Nothing gets past you, huh?'

'Am I gonna get the truth?'

'No,' Friesen says bluntly.

King believes him, so switches tracks. 'You said there's a way up. Is there a way down?'

'Haven't found out yet. That's why I told you to hold on.'

Panicked, battling sensory overload, King grips the door handle with white knuckles. 'And then...?'

'You feel like shit,' Friesen says, 'but I feel okay. And I guarantee you the men down there feel worse than you. So I say we take the opportunity we've been given, try to level the score.'

'I'm not gonna be much use.'

'I've got a trick or two up my sleeve.'

King faces forward as if concreted in place. The mouth of the crepuscular cave and the darkness within makes it feel like they're sitting inside a cannon, about to be shot out. The view of the Andes is surreal, framed by the cave walls around the entrance. A picture-perfect snapshot of staggering snow-capped mountains. Vicious wind howls in like a bad omen.

Even Friesen's jumpy.

For the first time since King met him, the man's voice wobbles as he asks, 'You holding on?'

King just grunts.

Friesen toes the accelerator and they inch forward toward the mouth. It's like they're riding the most dangerous rollercoaster ever conceived, seconds out from the trademark stomach drop.

King thought he was beyond fear.

But this is hell.

'If I'm wrong about this,' Friesen says right before they drop, 'I'm sorry.'

He taps the accelerator once more, the front wheels rumble over the lip of the cave, and the hood swings down in line with the slope.

The sudden wind is like a battering ram, and the acceleration smashes King back in his seat. He holds on for dear life.

Thanks to gravity, they do zero to sixty in a flash.

24

Two hundred harrowing feet into their descent, King thinks it might actually work.

Then they hit a rock at the wrong angle and bounce on the precipitous slope.

The whole vehicle goes airborne.

King pushes his feet hard into the footwell as his stomach lurches, trying to lock himself in place against the seat back. It works, but when they crash back down to earth, the front wheels slide on a patch of frozen dirt.

Friesen roars, '*Brace!*'

He wrestles with the steering wheel, gnashing his teeth together, animalistic. King catches a glimpse of the spook in his peripheral vision; Friesen barely looks human.

But thanks to his sheer determination, they don't flip.

Still, they skid uncontrollably, and the passenger side smashes into a boulder and hurtles them back in the other direction with a freshly crumpled door. The impact wobbles King's brain in his skull and he fights through the delirium and semi-consciousness to just *keep hold of the fucking door handle*. It's all he needs to do, yet his fingers can't seem to manage. Serious momentum throws him about, and all he can think is, *We could have just walked.*

He's furious at Friesen for having the courage to try this, but it's part of being pushed to your limits: your brain goes haywire. He's been uncontrollably angry in situations like these before, and he knows how to channel it constructively.

He directs it toward the Argentine troops below.

And a single thought comes to him as Friesen gains control of the jeep and continues speeding down the mountain: *Whatever they're expecting, it won't be this.*

The Argentines will be braced for a shootout, ready to potshot back and forth with King until they can outflank and surround their target. They'll know which instructions their bosses gave Reece Evans, and they'll expect the jeeps to be sabotaged, regardless of the climber's fate. A third vehicle won't even be in the realm of consideration.

King and Friesen are speeding down a slope facing south, while the Argentine troops are moving up the western face. There's a crucial slab of mountain shielding both parties from each other's view, which is critical. No matter how fast they're going, they're sitting ducks if the troops can draw a bead on them.

Friesen understands this, and as the most dangerous terrain recedes above them and the hillside begins to level out, he shouts, 'Ready?! Time to cut across.'

'They'll nail you as soon as we're in sight.'

'So I'll stay low.'

'*What?!*'

'Just shout directions. And don't fuck it up. Grab the rifle behind your seat.'

King understands what Friesen wants.

It's madness, but King's life has been madness for three straight years, and he might be the only person on earth who would sit across from Friesen and agree to such an insane plan. No matter how many times the spook lied to him, King suddenly feels begrudging respect.

He reaches back as Friesen pushes the jeep above sixty miles an hour, and fishes around the rear footwell until his fingers brush gunmetal. He lifts up the rifle, identifies it as an M16A4 with an ACOG sight and a fore grip, and he smiles: Christmas came early. Most of his joy is relief. He doesn't think he could throw punches if his life depended on it.

He only hopes he has the strength to keep the gun steady — there's little else he'll be useful for.

Friesen wrenches the wheel to the right, and they turn hard toward the western slope.

'Ready?' he asks as they surge diagonally down the volcano, moments from bursting into view of the Argentine troops.

But when King doesn't respond, Friesen looks over to find the rifle barrel inches from his face. He pales.

'You're not stupid,' he says.

What he means is, *If you shoot me, you'll be mince meat within seconds. You're not getting control of the vehicle if my body slumps across the wheel.*

'Not stupid,' King agrees, 'but not afraid, either. If you sold me out to Lars and whoever the hell is above Lars, then it doesn't matter whether I live or die here, because I'm dead anyway. So tell me the truth, or we'll both be mince meat. I'll know if you lie.'

It's true. Whether it's courtesy of his reaction speed, or just another genetic gift, he can read infinitesimal facial tics that others miss.

He knew Friesen was lying about taking Evans' phone, and he'll know if the man is lying now.

Friesen wrestles with the wheel; he can't take his eyes off the trail, or they'll skid off-course and flip. Wind batters him as he says through gritted teeth, 'I didn't sell you out. I reported our movements to Lars — that's it. I had my suspicions, and tried to get a confession out of him, but he gave me nothing. Steel trap.'

'Did you figure something like this would happen?'

'Maybe. I wasn't sure. As you can see, I prepared for it regardless.'

He's not lying, King can tell. It reveals exactly nothing, but the truth is often disappointing. The fact is, King won't know for sure whether Lars Crawford betrayed him until they're one-on-one and he can threaten to choke the life out of him.

There's nothing else to learn from Allan Friesen.

King pans his aim away, inching up in his seat so he can rest on the passenger door handle and lean out over the windowsill. Friesen relaxes a little, but not for long. The stretch of volcano that serves as a physical barrier between the two slopes falls away, and the western face opens up before them in all its panoramic glory.

King's now hanging his upper half out of the moving vehicle, so he can fire unobstructed without the windshield in the way. As soon as the western side of the edifice comes into view, he peers down the ACOG sight and does his very best not to topple out of the jeep. At this speed, over this terrain, the fall would smash him to pieces.

'Okay,' he yells, not quite able to believe that he's following Friesen's plan, '*down, now!*'

Friesen ducks out of sight, keeping both hands on the wheel.

Driving blind down the side of the highest volcano on the planet.

25

Turns out there was only milliseconds to spare.

The closest enemy is a single soldier — probably a scout — crouched behind a cluster of rocks. From a distance of maybe a hundred feet, the trooper whips his aim up and fires a couple of impulsive shots. He's incredibly well-trained. The bullets cut through the air over the top of the driver's door and whip past the space Friesen's skull occupied a second earlier. When they carry on, they narrowly miss King propped up on the passenger sill.

Thankfully, King's just as impeccably trained, if not more.

He smoothly swings the ACOG sight over to the enemy soldier as if it's just another day at the office. If he's tense and jumpy, his body won't let him make gentle micro-adjustments in milliseconds, and if he loses that capability, then his ungodly reaction speed is pointless. He needs every advantage here. Friesen can't see where he's going, they're bouncing and jolting on the unstable slope, and King's vision is blurry from the door rattling violently against the small of his back.

He exhales, letting it all go.

The scope's crosshairs wobble, tremble, lurch...

...and for the briefest moment in time, fall squarely on the Argentine's face.

King doesn't think, barely even registers it consciously.

He decides, and pulls the trigger.

The soldier's head snaps back and he spins into the residue of his own exit wound, crumpling unceremoniously to the rocks. King only just manages to register the kill before he swings his gaze forward and roars, '*Brake-left-turn!*' above the wind.

They didn't plan how they'd communicate in advance; they banked on the both of them being expertly-trained and accustomed to life-or-death situations. And it works.

Friesen responds almost unconsciously, stamping the brakes and twisting the wheel hard to the left, all while hunched over, staring at his feet. The jeep slides around the edge of a shallow ditch that would have crushed the hood beyond recognition and sent them both flying out of the vehicle. King figures the reinforced windshield frame would have cut him clean in half.

He grips the top of the windshield as Friesen blindly corrects course.

'Am I good?!' he roars.

'*Ten-seconds-faster-then-slow-and-right-turn,*' King shouts, so fast that it sounds like one long word.

Instructions delivered, he turns back to the slope, only a few seconds after killing the first soldier.

Another pair of Argentines have surged to their feet at the sight of the speeding jeep, rising from cover. They're taking careful aim; King takes less careful aim. He half-guesses where the crosshairs will land when he squeezes the trigger, then pulls.

The guy on the left goes down in a spray of blood before either of the pair can get a shot off.

It spooks the survivor into throwing himself down. It's the wrong decision; King only catches a flash of the guy's profile, but he sees that the man's aim had swung on target before he ducked. If the soldier simply pulled the trigger, King would be dead.

It's a harrowing thought, no matter how brief.

In the background, Friesen follows instructions. He leans on the accelerator as he counts to ten, the wheel shaking in his calloused palms, and he fights to hold his nerve and resist taking a peek. When he hits the allotted time, he taps the brakes and steers right. He has no idea how far to turn, but when the wheel hits a certain position, King yells, '*That's enough! Up!*'

Friesen straightens the wheel and lurches upright. Finally, they're facing horizontally across the slope, the windshield's bulletproof glass protecting the driver's seat from gunfire. Sure enough, the surviving soldier who ducked behind cover springs back up and fires an instinctive three-round burst. All the bullets deflect off the windshield, barely chipping the bulletproof glass.

King leans horizontally out of the jeep, takes careful aim, and fires one shot.

A third body sprawls onto the rocks.

King feels it now: the surge of mental power. It hits him hard, in a beautiful wave, and all his fatigue is forgotten.

He's only experienced the sensation a handful of times in his life, times where his predicament grew so dire that he was sure there was no coming back. When he's able to turn things around in the face of certain doom, it's a rush like no other. Up at their high camp, looking down on the approaching forces without a morsel of energy left, he was convinced he was dead, certain it was only a matter of time.

Now three of his enemies lie dead in less than a minute, and momentum's building, and even at a slightly lower altitude he can feel the extra oxygen in the air, and it's glorious, and maybe everything's going to be okay and he'll make it back to the life he loves...

Then they hit a bump.

It's nothing major, just a larger-than-usual jolt that runs up through the chassis as they bounce over a bunch of rocks, but King lifted his foot off the passenger seat at just the wrong time to adjust his position.

Next thing he knows, he's falling.

He slides off the sill, out of the vehicle. His legs are all that remain inside. As talented as he is, he can't defy the laws of physics, and gravity pushes him down, spilling him head over heels...

He sees the world upside-down, then the rocky slope rushes toward his unprotected skull.

He's about to be dumped on his head at fifty miles an hour.

Unsurvivable.

Then a hand snatches his ankle — his lower legs are all that remain in the jeep — and his descent stops violently. In a flash, he loses his grip on the M16 and it flies away.

A sharp rock, like a miniature pyramid, whistles past inches below his head. If it made contact, it would have cleaved his skull in two.

King dangles upside-down, the backs of his knees hooked over the sill.

Allan Friesen holds him in place with one hand and steers with the other. Bullets crack off the reinforced windshield as King flails his arms uselessly.

He's about to scream at Friesen to slow down so he can perform a sit-up and slide back into the jeep, but another pair of silhouettes clad in snow-coloured camouflage enter his inverted field of view. They're mere feet away, perched lower than King's head in a small, shallow basin a little further down the slope.

In a split second, King assesses angles and makes a call.

It's a crazier plan than anything they've already done.

But he follows through anyway, because if he stays put, he's just an upside-down piñata, at the mercy of their automatic gunfire.

Taking a deep breath, he blindly kicks Friesen's hand off his ankle.

Without anything securing him to the jeep, he falls. If he lands on rocks, he's dead.

He doesn't.

He lands on top of the enemy soldiers.

26

Instead of using his plummeting skull as a battering ram and delivering himself permanent brain damage in the process, he manages to bring his arms up to protect himself.

He uses them to break at least *some* of his fall.

He isn't sure where he makes contact with their bodies, but the soldiers' collective four hundred or so pounds serve as a far better landing pad than the hard volcanic edifice.

It's still brutal.

Out of the three of them, no one comes out of the collision in better shape than the others. Sure, King's bodyweight drives them to the ground and he comes down in an ungainly heap on top of them, crushing them into the rocks, but in the process he lands with all his weight on one arm, and he feels it go dead beneath him. His face hits the freezing dirt. The impact scrapes skin off one cheek and squashes his nose to one side. He can't even tell if it's broken, the sensory overload is so extreme. He rolls off the men without control and lands with all his weight on the small of his back.

It's a miracle it doesn't paralyse him.

When he sits up, he's hurting bad.

So are they.

He can't imagine what they just experienced. One moment they thought it was their lucky day, getting ready to pounce as the jeep sped toward them, and the next moment a two hundred and twenty pound man tumbled backwards out of the speeding vehicle and came down on top of them with enough force to concuss the both of them.

King's concussed, too; he didn't fare any better.

But in some twisted way, the previous day made him accustomed to feeling like shit, and clearly these men are still grappling with the altitude. They're slow to their feet, snatching weakly for their weapons, disoriented.

He's faster than them.

One of them lunges for the FN FAL rifle he was holding before King landed on him and smashed it from his hands. It's all a blur, but King surges to his feet and barrels over to the guy before his gloved fingertips brush the gunmetal. Still in motion, King jerks his left foot forward, kicking the rifle out of reach, then uses his momentum to swing his right knee for the heavens, as if trying to split the sky.

Instead he splits the soldier's unprotected face.

The man's visor is up, so his helmet only serves to frame his delicate facial bones. King's knee lands with a gruesome *crack* and the guy splays back, hands flying to his face in an instinctive effort to hold his broken bones together. He's still conscious, but no longer a problem.

He couldn't keep fighting if his life depended on it.

Which it does.

The second soldier somehow kept a fumbling hold on his weapon, but the collision and the fall spun the rifle in his hands, so it took a crucial second or two to correct his grip. He's fixed it by now. Still, it takes another crucial second to lock his aim on target, and by that point King's right there in his face.

As the man raises his gun, King grabs the underside of the barrel and wrenches the whole thing skyward. The soldier wasn't expecting it. He impulsively trigger-pulls, but it's too late: the rifle's now aimed straight up in the air. A couple of shots blast harmlessly overhead, then King seizes hold of the weapon with both hands to pin it in place. As expected, the guy uses a burst of freakish strength, trying to wrestle the gun away. He should have forgotten all about it. Should have let go, ducked low, and knocked all the wind out of King by slamming a fist into his unprotected stomach.

But we don't see what's best, we see what we *think* is best, especially when success or failure often comes down to the decisions made in milliseconds.

It's this theory that King's career is built around. When battles are often random, with who lives and dies in an unexpected shootout usually dependent on fate, any advantage — even the slightest edge — is priceless. King was born with an edge, so the secret world took the plunge and invested millions upon millions of dollars in the development of a single covert operative. It's why King believed this expedition to Ojos del Salado was genuine. Of course they would spend this much to cart him to wherever they thought he'd evolve the fastest: they'd done it before. Black Force, essentially, is a cohort of obscenely overpriced solo assassins, who require expensive training and demand expensive payouts for their services.

Because they're the best and they know it.

All the money and time invested in King, all the focus on honing his reflexes and reaction speed, is precisely for situations like these.

The times where one man makes a good decision, but the other makes a slightly better one.

And then it's over.

The soldier doesn't see what he should do. Maybe after a couple of seconds wrestling for the rifle he would have, but it's too late to know. Point is, he makes the split-second mistake, and King doesn't. *King* is the one to release his hold on the rifle, to suddenly drop low and throw two violent uppercuts — left-right — into the soldier's groin.

The guy howls and falls to his knees, the damage unimaginable.

King simply catches the rifle, stands up to his fullest height, and fires two shots.

One in each man's head.

Their shouts die out, somewhat mercifully.

To an observer, it would have seemed like total, random chaos. Like King threw himself in the mix and only came out on top because he won a coin toss. But that's the way it always looks, and every time Jason King manages to get the upper hand.

You can't fluke hundreds of small victories.

King turns to face the jeep, which screeched to a halt a couple of dozen feet from the depression he tumbled into. He makes eye contact with Friesen in the driver's side mirror, and it's clear that the spook knows it wasn't random. You can't afford to rely on luck in the savage side of the world. There's a strange clarity in Friesen's eyes now, like he truly understands what King's made of, and if King still suspected a double cross, any notion of betrayal vanishes.

Friesen will fight with him and die with him.

Until they're off this mountain, they're brothers.

King vaults out of the depression, sprints to the jeep and leaps back into the passenger seat. 'Go.'

Friesen hits the gas.

They rocket forward.

27

There's a lull, if you can call it that.

Maybe thirty uninterrupted seconds in which they're not getting shot at, where the curvature of the terrain shields them from the enemies which lie further along the slope.

Compared to what came before, the half-minute is bliss.

Dead tired but somehow able to ignore it, King asks, 'Did you park in front of the dip to protect me from gunfire?'

He isn't quite able to believe it, and it's clear in his voice.

Friesen recognises his disbelief, and wryly smiles. 'It's like you're still surprised I haven't backstabbed you.'

'I think I trust you. But I thought I trusted Reece. So nothing much would shock me now.'

Hunched over the wheel, Friesen says, 'You sound right as rain.'

'I'm...'

King trails off. He hadn't given any thought to his condition, too focused on kill after kill after kill, but now, during a short lull in action, Friesen's words suddenly draw his attention to how he feels. As if Friesen made it happen, a giant wave of fatigue crashes over him. The sensation is so over-whelming that he literally sags in his seat.

Friesen doesn't notice; he's facing forward, zoned in as they crash over the terrain.

The spook goes on: 'It's a miracle you're alright, 'cause from what I scoped out, there's a cluster of them around this bend, and that's the last of them. Five, maybe six altogether, and then it's done. You've taken care of the scouts. You ready for—?'

But he must have sensed something, because he cuts himself off and flashes a look over, taking his eyes off their mad descent.

By that point, King lies slumped halfway down the seat, half his torso sliding into the footwell. Aware of what's happening, he can do nothing to stop it. A strange semi-consciousness falls over him as he fights against his brain's central governor. The same way a vehicle's governor auto-matically stops it from going above a certain speed, we all have a point where our mind says, *No more,* and shuts down our body. What's worse is that King had no inclination it was coming. Coming out the other side of what he just survived, he was high on his last reserves of adrenaline without realising, and the shift is as disorienting as it is unexpected.

He manages to mumble, 'I'm trying,' as he crumples in a heap and begins to hyperventilate.

Friesen stares down at him. The spook's face is twisted in a grimace.

'I know you're trying,' he says. 'I know.' He looks up, and the grimace tightens. 'Look, we're seconds out...'

In moments, they'll round the curve in the hillside and come into full view of the remaining hostiles. The soldiers in that squad — five or six men, Friesen said — will be the important ones, the guys who sent the scouts ahead. Included in their rank will be the commander, and all the murky answers about why this is happening lie between his ears. Without getting the guy in charge, this is all futile.

King wills his body to function. 'Just give me a few—'

'There isn't time.'

'Just wait,' King snarls, practically spitting the two syllables.

He tries to reach up and grip the sill of the passenger door, use it to drag himself back upright so at least he can try to aim his rifle when the two parties spot each other. Without him, Friesen's a sitting duck.

He raises his arm.

His muscles shake and his shoulder trembles and his wrist spasms. His fingers dangle uselessly, and he realises he can't even move the digits: perhaps the best indication of how little energy he has left.

Still, he fights and he fights and he fights.

No surrender, a voice in his head barks, but that doesn't matter when it feels like every inch that he raises his arm comes with another invisible weight on the back of his hand, forcing him down.

Down...

Down.

He slumps, folded in the footwell, and his vision blurs. Edges lose their hardness, and everything swims.

Friesen says, 'You're done.'

It's true.

He's done.

By this point, continuing to deny it would be dangerous ignorance.

So he uses the very last of his reserves to lower his chin in a nod.

'Okay,' Friesen says. 'Let's get out of here.'

He rips the wheel, and King feels the jeep turn hard beneath him. They veer away from the corner they were about to round, taking a straight shot down the slope.

Escaping with their lives, but no answers.

King feels his eyes closing. He isn't consciously doing it, and it's terrifying. He can't stop himself sinking into darkness.

He keeps fighting.

Always fighting...

But he fails.

The world slips away into woozy delirium.

28

Lars Crawford pulled two consecutive all-nighters as he hashed out the details of betraying Jason King.

Now, after nearly fifty hours without sleep, he stumbles into a windowless room burrowed deep in the bowels of the building that houses Christian West's Washington D.C. office. He walks over to a cheap blue sofa shoved up against one wall, flops down on it, and falls asleep in seconds.

The operation is live.

His work is done.

Ordinarily, he'd be right there in the control room, helping to lead his best active operative into the fray, but this time he would only be leading King like a lamb to the slaughter. He demanded to sit this one out, and, unexpectedly, "The Golden One" agreed.

Now Lars sleeps the sleep of the dead.

He's exhausted: physically, mentally, emotionally. Maybe even spiritually, although he's not particularly religious. He thought he was a man of principle, a man who believed in the words he spoke, but the moment Christian West demanded otherwise, he caved. Maybe he always knew he would. Perhaps he wouldn't have got into this messy business in the first place if he ever thought he'd truly take a moral stand.

Death scares him more than any decision he could make here on earth.

He's not ashamed to admit he's scared to die.

So if it's either him or King whose head is on the chopping block, that's an easy choice. And it helps him sleep now. He plunges into a deep, dreamless slumber.

He has no idea how much time passes.

Next thing he knows, someone's shaking him awake.

"Shaking" doesn't do it justice. The man looming over him is King's size, at least two hundred and twenty pounds, and he uses all of that power to grab Lars by the shoulders and heave him up and down in place. A headache instantly explodes to life, and Lars feels his brain rattle in his skull, his eyes in their sockets.

'Stop!' he roars. 'What are you *doing*?!'

He hates physical confrontation.

It's why he sits behind a desk and tells the real killers what to do.

The guy stops shaking him, and Lars makes out his face. It's not King, but that's no relief, because Lars recognises the balaclava with the skull spray-painted on it, and quickly identifies the man. He doesn't know his name, has never even seen his face, but West has used this method before to intimidate Lars.

It always works.

You think you'd get used to it, but somehow it only gets worse each time.

Then again, Lars thinks, *everything Christian does, works.*

Sure enough, when the balaclava speaks, it's not the

voice of the man behind the mask. It's the voice of "The Golden One," projected from a small speaker behind the coarse wool. There's a microphone there, too, so that Lars can converse with West. The hulking enforcer serves as his mouthpiece, a body that can use force where Christian never would.

'You botched it,' West says through the speaker as the big man looms over Lars. The effect is as disorienting as it is terrifying. 'You should have told Reece to RPG his tent like I ordered. You made him use a knife instead and he fucked it up. Now he's dead, along with half of Enzo's men. What are you going to do about it, Lars?'

It's perhaps the most important question Lars Crawford has ever been asked.

If he gets the answer wrong, the mute enforcer will beat him to death in this backroom.

He's no fool; he knows what's on the line.

Lars blinks, still pinned to the sofa on his back. 'Uh ... where's Enzo now? Where's the other half of his men?'

'They're up at the camp King abandoned after he stabbed Reece to death.'

Lars' heart thuds, vibrating his chest wall. 'Where's Friesen?'

'With King.'

'What?'

'Why is that a surprise?' the voice hisses through the tinny speaker. 'He wasn't your hitman. He damn well *should've* been.'

'He wouldn't have done it,' Lars says frantically. The skull mask hovers above him, expressionless. 'Friesen's got a hell of a lot more in common with King than he does with us.'

'He was happy to give you updates,' West says, doubtful. 'He must have known what was coming. He didn't protest.'

'I'm sure he had a hunch. But if I'd asked him to be the one to do it, he would have grit his teeth, accepted, then changed his mind when it was time to pull the trigger.'

'I don't let people change their minds.'

'Some choose death over dishonour.'

Silence.

Then West says, 'Well, the pair of them fled instead of shooting it out with Enzo. I don't blame them. The guy's loco, and his file suggests he's every bit as talented as King. I need you to—'

'*Just let me come upstairs!*' Lars yells uncontrollably. He can't help himself; the pressure on his shoulders is immense as the enforcer pins him to the sofa. He feels his desperation mount. 'Let's talk face to face, Christian.'

Through the speaker, West tuts. 'Afraid not. You've lost privileges. You don't get to see me until you fix this. I'll have my man there watch over you.'

How am I going to fix it? Lars laments. *You want my operatives dead, and I dedicated my life to making them unkillable.*

But, although some *do* choose death over dishonour, he sure isn't one of them. So he asks, 'What do you want, exactly?'

'Order King to standby. That way Enzo can catch him. King trusts you.'

'Not anymore,' Lars mutters. 'I doubt he trusts anyone now.'

'Then get creative. But you'd better hold him up, or I'll have you beaten to death on that shitty sofa. You've got a phone on you. Get to work.'

There's an audible click and Lars knows West won't hear anything else he has to say.

The enforcer finally releases him, but only backs up a few steps, hovering like a nightmarish apparition in one corner of the room.

Lars sits up, hands trembling, and gently takes out his phone.

He stares at it for a couple of seconds before his survival instinct takes control and he starts frantically making calls to Copiapó.

29

King isn't unconscious for long.

But he's *semi*-conscious for hours.

Given the circumstances, it scares him to his core. When he first swims back to reality, he manages to peel himself out of the footwell, crawling up into the passenger seat, and the following hours pass in a fever dream. Friesen says nothing, just drives. It's about all the spook can manage. He's compromised, too, exhausted from the time spent at altitude and the massive stress of the initial descent. Sure, he wasn't fighting or shooting or killing, but adrenaline dumps are largely the same.

They sap everything from you.

It's a monastic drive down out of the Andes and across the Atacama Desert. King knows it's nearly half a day back to Copiapó, but it sure doesn't feel that way. To him, it's just a blur of timeless motion. On one hand, it seems like minutes, and on the other, like days.

But they arrive.

It's late afternoon by the time the small city appears as a speck on the horizon, the windswept plains shimmering in grey light. King straightens a little in his seat. Moving his body feels like dragging around a two hundred and twenty pound block of concrete.

'We heading back to the plane?' he asks, the first words spoken between them in hours.

'I am,' Friesen says. 'I'll drop you in town so you can hole up for a couple of days. Then I'll press on.'

King hesitates. 'What if I don't want that?'

Friesen half-smirks. 'Well, I can't force you. You made that clear when we landed.'

'I'm a little tireder now.'

'Still...' A couple of seconds go by. 'Anyway, I suggest you take my advice. It's your choice, but if I were you I wouldn't step foot on a U.S. aircraft until I give the green light.'

King stares. 'If they're behind it, they'll kill you.'

Friesen shrugs. 'Then at least you'll know it's time to disappear. You don't hear from me, you become a ghost.'

'No,' King says. 'I'm not making you do that. You owe me nothing.'

'You're not making me do a damn thing.'

'Then why are you *choosing* it? We could both vanish, right here, right now. Go our separate ways, leave this bull-shit behind...'

Friesen slowly shakes his head. 'Afraid not, brother. I have a wife. A little girl.'

'You're no good to them dead.'

'I'm no good to them excommunicated. So it doesn't matter either way. At least this way, I get some answers.'

'Answers?' King scoffs. 'Those in charge will just shoot you.'

'If it's them.'

'You think it is,' King says. 'It's why you made up that crap about Reece's phone, about his gambling debts. You covered for them instinctively, because you thought they told Reece to do it, and you didn't want me to know that.'

He isn't expecting a reply.

It shocks him when Friesen says, 'You got me.'

King studies the man's face. 'What are you, exactly? It's like you've got a foot on either side of the line. You had a serious hunch they were going to try to take me out. Maybe you even knew for sure. But they didn't ask you to do it — why? You'd have refused? It would have been a whole lot easier to warn me about what was coming than to fight alongside me after it happened.'

'Conditioning,' Friesen says as Copiapó looms ahead.

'What?'

'I've done six years with the Special Activities Center. Above all else, they teach you to obey. It's in my DNA by this point. Sometimes you don't know why, but you do what you're told. I'm not a strategist. I can't see the long-term effects of the hits I carry out. I just point and shoot.' He pauses a moment, as if he's never voiced it that way before. Maybe he's never even *thought* like that. 'So, yeah, I knew what they were going to do, even though they didn't explicitly say it. I figured I'd just sit back and look the other way. I put the jeep in that cave as a fallback for *me,* not for *us.* Then I saw it playing out, and ... I changed my mind.'

'You ever done that before?'

'No.'

'There'll be consequences.'

'I already weighed that up before I decided.'

King knows what he's talking about. He's been there. 'You accepted the worst-case scenario?'

'A good soldier would take a bullet for the man beside him,' Friesen says softly. 'How is this any different? Besides the fact the bullet's coming later, from my own superiors.'

30

Emotion wells in King's chest as he listens to Friesen.

A life spent operating solo in the shadows sometimes makes him forget what people are capable of doing for each other. He clamps a hand down on the man's shoulder. 'You don't know there's a bullet coming.'

'Yesterday you name-dropped Lars Crawford,' Friesen says. 'You know him well?'

'He's my handler.'

'You trust him?'

King thinks about it. 'He's never done anything to suggest I shouldn't.'

'I trust him, too. But I don't know who he works for. I don't know to what extent he's a puppet.'

'Me neither. I doubt we ever will.'

Friesen's eyes harden, his gaze becoming thunder. 'I'll find out.'

He veers the jeep west just before they hit the edge of Copiapó, onto an unpaved track that leads them away from the arterial main road. King understands why — too many potential witnesses if they drive through the heart of town. Still, despite the fact he's in no state to interact with strangers, he's disappointed. He wanted another stop at the food truck for some *pan con chicharrón*, more to see the little boy again than to catch a break from the MREs he's been forcing down.

He doesn't care about eating bland field rations.

For some strange reason, he just wants to speak with David. The kid was a flash of normalcy in the middle of the whirlwind.

But it's a stupid idea, especially considering the Argentine soldiers likely made their way to Ojos del Salado from the Chilean side. They must have passed through Copiapó, and there's no telling if any men lingered behind.

So, low profile.

King forgets the pork and potato and young David's hilarious version of English. He lets Friesen drive him to the outskirts of the city, where they plunge into a rundown, largely abandoned stretch that runs parallel to the Copiapó River. They go off-road and bounce across a dusty block of land until they're parked a few hundred feet behind a remote gas station.

Ahead lies a shipping container, slapped down between desert shrubs like a strange art installation.

'It's the gas station's,' Friesen explains before King can ask. 'The owner plans to use it for storage, but for now it's empty. I negotiated with him on my first trip here. He's not gonna look inside it for the next week or so. I kicked him a bit of cash.'

'Your fallback?' King asks. 'In case it turned out you were the one they wanted gone?'

'Uh-huh. There's a mattress in there, some water, some

more MREs. But you've got enough supplies on you anyway — training camp didn't last very long, huh?'

'You sure made use of the time we had.'

'Yeah,' Friesen says slowly. He's clearly aware of the elephant in the room: he was the one who sapped King's energy, giving Reece the opportunity to pounce. 'How you feeling now?'

'Strange.'

It's the only way King can think of putting it. Copiapó's only twelve hundred feet above sea level, meaning they descended nineteen thousand feet over the course of the drive back. Each breath now floods him with oxygen, like there's a mask over his face connected to a bottle of the stuff, but that doesn't mean he's instantly cured. Although it's heavenly each time he inhales, he's aware that the last twenty-four hours destroyed him. Besides the times he suffered serious injuries in the field, Ojos del Salado pushed him closer to the edge than he's ever been.

It takes time to crawl back from that edge.

His central nervous system is fried, and every movement is like fighting through quicksand.

'I get it,' Friesen says, even though King never tried to explain. 'You're going to need a couple of days, minimum — even if you're the fittest person on earth, which you damn well could be.'

King shifts subtly in his seat. 'So this is it?'

'For us, it is. Maybe I'll see you round.'

'We both know that's not gonna happen. Even if we make it through.'

Friesen stares off into space and tilts his head in a slow nod of acceptance. 'Yeah. But, uh...' He meets King's gaze. 'I appreciate the time I got to spend with you. You've got something that's ... well, it's addictive to be around. I'll leave it at that.'

King gets the sense that the spook usually keeps his cards pretty close to his chest. It makes Friesen uncomfortable, opening up like that.

But King doesn't have time to appreciate the admission, because what Friesen said makes him realise why the upper echelon needed Reece Evans. It didn't make sense that they pulled in an inexperienced mountain climber to try to assassinate the most dangerous covert operative alive.

Now it does.

Friesen must notice King's expression change. 'What?'

'Nothing major. But I just put two and two together. I know why they used Reece.'

'That's been doing my head in. Care to enlighten me?'

'It'd sound too egotistical if I did. You'll figure it out. Or Lars will tell you.' King outstretches a hand. 'Thank you for everything.'

Friesen accepts the handshake. 'Just doing my job.'

King pops the door, steps down into the dust, and lifts his pack off the rear seats. It feels like it weighs a ton. He struggles with it as he limps slowly away from the jeep. He thought that hours of semi-consciousness would revive him, but he's not out of the woods yet.

Again, Friesen's right.

Just before he hobbles out of earshot, he looks back. Friesen sits behind the wheel, face blank. He's a consummate professional, through and through, conserving his energy wherever possible.

'You know,' King calls out, 'if they paired us up in the beginning, we'd have done some serious damage over the years.'

Friesen's mouth curls from a hard line up into a smile.

'I was thinking the same thing, brother,' he calls back. 'Take care of yourself.'

'I'll wait for your call.'

King turns away, creaks the shipping container's door open, and stumbles into the darkness within.

31

Allan Friesen drives northwest with a lump in his throat.

Headed for *Aeropuerto Copiapó*.

He's scared, but that's normal. He's spent most of his career scared, most of his *life* scared. Doesn't change a thing. He believes that living nobly is about doing the things you're supposed to do, whether you feel like them or not. This philosophy shaped his nine-year journey from an Army private with no rank insignia — an E-1 "fuzzie" — to the very top of the CIA's Special Activities Center. Now it might carry him to his death, but that's okay.

Better an honourable death than a miserable life.

Nevertheless, the fear is real. He reaches the airport, passes through a checkpoint without resistance, and drives straight to the runway he's looking for.

The Globemaster sits waiting.

As he knew it would be.

The rear ramp descends to reveal three men. It's the same pilot, but the co-pilot and loadmaster are new: their predecessors lie dead in a ditch on Ojos del

Salado. The fresh faces are Caucasian, almost certainly American. They must have been pulled from some black site in a neighbouring country. Sometimes Friesen forgets just how fast the military industrial complex can move.

He gets out of the jeep and collects his gear, leaving it for the loadmaster to drive into the plane. Then he walks slowly up the ramp into the cargo compartment.

He passes briefly by the pilot.

The rugged man takes one look at him and says, 'You're in deep—'

'Yeah, yeah,' Friesen mutters, cutting him off. 'I didn't kill your buddies, if that's what you're thinking.'

The pilot squares up, preventing Friesen from passing by. The co-pilot and the loadmaster scurry down the ramp behind him.

Tension hangs thick in the air.

The pilot leans in close. 'I don't believe a fucking word that comes out of your mouth.'

Friesen leans in closer. 'And what exactly are you planning to do about that?'

A sudden pang of worry creases the man's face, and he takes a step back. We may think we're above the primal hierarchy, but everyone instantly knows who the most dangerous man in the room is. The pilot realises it, and puts some space between himself and Friesen's fists.

But he has *some* leverage. 'I'm not flying you anywhere. Get out of here.'

'My bosses want me home,' Friesen says plainly. 'Probably to do what you want to do to me. So you can either deliver me to them or piss them off. I don't give a shit.'

He sits on one of the hard metal seats, leans back, and closes his eyes. It's not a show. He's genuinely exhausted, and he knows they won't drag him off the plane. Even if they leave him here, he needs sleep.

But fifteen minutes later, he feels the Globemaster rumble beneath him as it labours into motion.

They blast down the runway and lift into the darkening sky.

32

The next morning...

Vicente Herrero owns and operates a dilapidated gas station in the strange no-man's-land where Copiapó becomes the Atacama Desert.

On a good day, he gets ten customers.

If he's really lucky, someone will buy a snack or a drink instead of just pumping and paying — there's barely any profit in the fuel. On those days, he's ecstatic.

Today, he's unlucky.

He watches from behind the counter with a lump in his throat as a police cruiser coasts to a halt beside the rusting pumps. A large cop peels himself out from behind the wheel and strides toward the building, ignoring the nozzles. So he's not here for gas, which means...

His boots thud on the dusty concrete until he grows close enough for Herrero to make out the green patch on his uniform: it reads *Carabineros de Chile.*

Thanks to his murky past, Herrero knows the names and

faces of all the Carabiniers — Chile's national law enforce-
ment — who reside in Copiapó. This guy isn't one of them.

Which makes it very serious.

The cop from out of town steps into the store; a bell
above the grimy glass door jangles. He pans his gaze
slowly across the shelves as if it isn't obvious that
Herrero is the only person here. Then he approaches the
counter.

Herrero says nothing. He's found it's best to just shut up
and let them do whatever they're going to do.

The policeman stops inches from the counter, stares at
Herrero, and says, 'You are blessed,' in Spanish.

Herrero doesn't feel blessed. '¿Lo estoy?'

Am I?

'Oh, yes. If I were you, I'd cry tears of relief and gratitude
tonight.'

Herrero shifts his weight to the other foot. The back of
his neck grows hot. His discomfort is palpable, and the big
cop notices. It brings a smile to the man's face.

'I guess to be grateful, you must know why,' he says. 'For-
tunately, I'm in a good mood.'

Herrero keeps his expression blank.

'You are hiding a murderous American savage up the
back of your property.'

'I—'

The cop holds up a hand. 'If you lie, your blessings will
fall away. You don't need to tell the truth either. You just
need to listen.'

Herrero hesitates, but the pressure gets to him. He nods
his understanding.

'You know why it's your lucky day?'

Herrero shakes his head.

'Because if it was any other American pig back there,'

the cop says, 'I would have already shot you dead, right where you stand.'

To make his point, he rips his Ruger P90 sidearm from its holster and aims it square between Herrero's eyes.

Herrero's knees wobble, and overwhelming fear makes him instantly compliant.

The cop tucks his piece away. 'But, unfortunately, it's not just any American pig. It's perhaps the most dangerous American pig alive. So if we take care of you, then go shoot up that shipping container out back, chances are we won't accomplish shit — we'll only pay for it with our lives.' He shrugs. 'Anyway, not my problem — the Argentines have promised to take care of this guy. So I've got a task for you.'

Whatever the cop says, Herrero will comply. He knows that already, his legs trembling beneath him as he remembers the dark maw of the Ruger.

'Y-yes?' he stammers.

'Once I leave, go out back and knock on the container. Tell the American about the murders.'

Herrero doesn't respond, still slack-jawed. As confusing a request as it is, it's far simpler than he expected. 'What murders? The taqueria kid and his mother? And, wait, that's all you want?'

'That's all I want,' the cop assures. 'Like I said, you are blessed.'

'Okay.' Maybe he actually is.

'The boy's name is David. The mother's is Julieta.'

'Okay.'

Herrero doesn't want to push his luck. He stays as still as possible, says as little as possible. The cop takes a final look at him, then turns on his heel and leaves as quickly as he arrives. Herrero waits for the cruiser to peel away before he lurches out from behind the counter and runs down a corridor marked STAFF ONLY. He bursts out into a desolate stretch of desert riddled with thick shrubs, and weaves between them as he makes fast for the shipping container.

Breathing hard, desperate to do exactly as instructed, he slams a fist twice on the big door.

It's like reality glitches. The door swings open so fast he hardly sees it, and next thing he knows there's another pistol aimed at his forehead. Herrero isn't a soldier or a cop — doesn't even claim to be a tough guy — so although his past life is morally contentious, he doesn't have any experience in this world of constant threats. But he knows one thing: he's never seen a man move so fast, never witnessed someone so *ready*. He knows he could die in the next instant; the American won't hesitate.

A low voice floats from the gloom. 'What?'

The pistol barrel doesn't waver a millimetre.

'I sorry,' Herrero stammers in broken English. 'I know I promise to stay away. But something you need to know.'

'Go on.'

Draped in shadow, Herrero sees fierce blue eyes set in a face that would be considered model good-looking if its expression weren't so severe and its complexion so wind-battered. The guy looks like the Terminator, but more hand-some (under the battle scars, at least.) Herrero never believed these people were real. It nearly spooks him into silence, but he manages to press forward.

'Do you know taqueria? Food truck?'

Those brilliant cerulean eyes flare.

No answer.

'You do, yes?' Herrero knows he must, for news of the murders to mean anything.

Finally the huge American says, 'Yes.'

Herrero makes to reveal what he knows, but finds he

can't. The stranger's stare is the most thunderous gaze he's ever witnessed, and he wilts before it. Terrified, no longer considering the cop's wishes, he starts to back away.

'Tell me,' the American orders.

The pistol hasn't gone anywhere.

Herrero holds up his hands. 'Please. Just ... go see what happen.'

'I don't have the freedom to do that,' the low voice says. 'Tell me now.'

Herrero reaches the tipping point and the floodgates open. 'Yesterday morning ... some soldiers move through city. We no see before. We no know who they are. They hurt some people. They strangle little boy ... David? And also strangle mother, Julieta. Both dead. Then soldiers leave for mountains.'

Nothing really changes in the American's face, but somehow, at the same time, his whole demeanour shifts. Herrero thought he'd felt pure terror before, but now he realises that all those times pale in comparison to what he feels now. The strange man in the shipping container seems otherworldly, his fury palpable, as if his rage is a supercharger. Herrero has never seen anything like it.

'Understood,' the American says, his voice so deep, so angry. 'Go.'

Herrero turns and runs back to the gas station.

33

W hen you fly in on a CIA-owned Globemaster, you get to avoid the civilian limits for travelling with cash.

King has fifty thousand USD in Benjamin Franklins slotted in a concealed compartment at the bottom of his pack. He's carted the money around for so long, sometimes he forgets it exists. There's never been reason to use it, but he's waiting for the day where an op goes sick and wrong and he loses access to the financial might of the military industrial complex.

It's a contingency against his worst nightmare: being stuck in hostile territory with no resources.

Now he takes out one of the five stacks — ten thousand USD — and slings his pack over his shoulder. Clipped to the duffel is a long bag for storing full-sized rifles: the FN FAL he stripped off one of the Argentines rests within.

He leaves the shipping container without a second thought.

He slept the deepest sleep imaginable the night before, and when he woke this morning, he realised Friesen had been wrong. King didn't need forty-eight hours to recover. He woke with a functioning central nervous system, his body so used to regularly healing massive physical damage that it fixed the worst of it overnight. His bones still hurt and his muscles ached like crazy, but that was all superficial. It no longer felt like he was moving through quicksand wearing ankle weights, and he'd been planning his departure from Copiapó when the guy who owned the gas station came labouring up to the container.

King had heard him approaching a solid twenty seconds before he knocked.

As he heard the news the man shared, his heart sank.

Now he strides powerfully for the main road, head spinning with fury. He can't detach from the anger, can't process it or heal from it.

He can only use it.

He makes it to the central avenue, emerging right where he planned to, and when he looks north he sees exactly what he expects to see.

Police tape around the food truck.

Cops crawling all over it.

He doesn't need to investigate, doesn't need to see the bodies or get a closer look. He knows it's true. The little guy and his mother are dead. Maybe it was a deliberate ploy to draw King out, or maybe it was sheer coincidence.

It really doesn't matter either way.

King doesn't give a shit if it's a trap. He equally doesn't care whether the soldier who killed David and Julieta was one of his victims the day before. He slaughtered half the Argentinian posse, so it's fifty-fifty odds whether the killer is still alive, and that's not good enough.

Therefore, the rest of them need to go.

Simple as that.

King strides south, along the road that runs all the way out of town, across the desert, and into the mountains. As he walks, a thought strikes him.

Of course it's a trap.

Otherwise, why the hell would the gas station owner have bothered telling him?

It's obvious now: the guy was told to bait King, send him charging back to the Andes. In fact, it's so obvious that it makes King doubt himself, because in different circumstances he would have put that together in two seconds flat. He must still be compromised mentally, his short-term processing power impeded. Doubt starts to seep in, but he distracts himself by flagging down the first four-wheel drive that passes by.

Mood follows action, he reminds himself as the vehicle pulls to the sandy shoulder beside him. If he's too busy to second-guess himself, there simply won't be time for hesitation.

The 4WD he hailed is a Toyota Hilux pickup with a metal bed, at least ten years old, the whole chassis caked in dust. A massive dent distorts the rear passenger door — the damage must be recent, because duct tape holds together the lower half of the window above the indentation.

King thanks his lucky stars, and hopes the driver's more likely to want to alleviate himself of the rust-bucket.

The driver's window lowers as the guy behind the wheel works the manual crank. He wrestles the pane two-thirds of the way down before he gives up and sticks his head out through the gap. '¿Qué?'

He's maybe forty, deeply tanned, with a thick black beard.

'English?' King asks.

The man shakes his head.

King holds up the stack of cash. The driver doesn't need English to identify Benjamin Franklin on the first note.

'Ten thousand U.S. Dollars,' King says.

No translation necessary.

The man's eyes widen. 'Why?'

King points to the car.

No debate required. It would be more than a year's wages here in Chile, far more than the driver could hope to make selling the Hilux to a used-car dealer. He quite literally scrambles out, shoving the door outward in his haste, like the offer might expire at any moment. He quickly collects an armful of possessions off the rear seats, then steps away. He doesn't blink. He stares at the money as if it might disappear.

King hands the stack over.

The guy takes the cash in a shaking hand.

King throws his own huge duffel in the back, then gets behind the wheel and roars away.

34

Twelve hours have passed since Lars first stumbled into this backroom for a power-nap.

The enforcer in the corner only left once — to fetch him food and water — and has otherwise stood deathly still like an automaton, watching Lars squirm from behind the skull mask.

Lars became delirious hours ago, and now reality no longer feels real.

When the phone rings in his hand, he doesn't quite believe it.

He answers softly, unable to help sounding detached. 'Yes?'

'King's heading back to the mountains,' Christian West says. 'Enzo will take care of him. Your work's done. Good job.'

Lars hears the words, but they hardly mean anything. He's been stressed for so long that it's fried his brain. He lifts his gaze slowly to the brute in the corner. 'Are ... you going to kill me?'

A sharp laugh. 'Don't be stupid,' West says. 'I need you.'

'If I asked you to,' Lars says, 'would you?'

Silence.

West asks, 'Are you suicidal?'

'I—'

'Answer the question.'

'I don't know. I hate this, Christian. What if Enzo isn't good enough to get the job done? What then?'

'He's good enough. We trained his father.'

'What?'

'Operation Condor. Enzo's dad was critical to the state terror we inflicted in Argentina. The dirty bastard passed those lessons down to his son, along with ... well, let's just say the old man had PTSD and leave it at that. Anyway — I checked Enzo's file and he's as legit as they come. Hell, once Black Force is dead, maybe he can be your next project, huh? I might have use for a division without morals.'

Lars read Enzo's file, too, and concluded that, although the guy's clearly talented, "sadistic and psychopathic" actually understates how evil he is.

'I'm good,' he says.

Another laugh. 'If I say that's what you're doing, it's what you're doing.'

'So that's an order?'

'We'll see.'

'And as for now...?'

'I don't need you. Good call with Herrero. Get out of here.'

'Should I come upstairs so we can strategise what comes after King's death?'

'I don't need you,' West repeats, firmer this time. 'When King's out of the picture, we'll do the same thing to Will Slater. He's a legitimate alcoholic — it'll be easier with him.'

Lars sits still, his muscles aching from lack of movement, taking a moment. Then he says, 'Understood.'

'Go home. I'll contact you when it's done.'

The moment West hangs up, the enforcer in the skull mask turns on his heel and leaves the room. For the first time in half a day, Lars is alone, unmonitored, and he hangs his head and suppresses tears of relief.

After a spell, he rises and mopes out of the building.

He regrets everything.

35

Enzo takes the call at twenty thousand feet.

He stands at the edge of the precipice, overlooking a staggering swathe of the Andes, the mountain range impossibly severe. Behind him sit the two jeeps with their shredded tyres and the small collection of tents erected for the soft Americans. Two of his surviving men lie in those tents now, equally soft, crippled by horrifying altitude sickness after such a rapid ascent. There's a chance they'll come good, but they most likely won't be functional until they've descended. Enzo has experience in the Andes, and knows if they get HAPE (a vicious build-up of fluid in the lungs), they may well die.

He doesn't much care.

If they can't hack it, that's their problem, and he received no orders to follow the fleeing Americans down the volcano. Until he does, they'll stay put, the safety of his men be damned.

Enzo is a professional and a professional does precisely what he's told.

For example, he was told to expect a call from an

unimaginably powerful figure up north, so now he answers the blocky sat phone in English. 'Hello?'

'Is this Enzo?' The voice is deep, husky, authoritative.

'Speaking.'

'Enzo, my name is Christian.'

'Hello, Christian.'

'May I share something with you?'

'Sure.'

'Only nine people on earth know my name. You're now the tenth.'

'Why?' Enzo stares out across the mountains. 'You didn't have to do that.'

'But I wanted to,' Christian says. 'I need you to understand how much I'm depending on you for what's to come. You see, I've taken a gamble, making the decision to eliminate my own countrymen. It's the right decision, but it's a risk. I opted for Ojos del Salado as the battleground primarily because I read your file and know of your talents. I think you are every bit as skilled as the man I want dead. His name is Jason King. He—'

'Christian?' Enzo interjects.

'Yes?'

'I tell the truth. I do not hide my failures. There are three dead men up here. None of them are this man, King. The way they died ... they were not talented or skilled. The one who killed half my men ... he was talented. He was skilled. And he got away. I will not lie to you.'

Enzo swears he hears the exhale of a smile through the phone.

'You're a good man,' Christian says. 'But don't worry. I know King got away. I also know he's coming back.'

Enzo stiffens. 'Why?'

'There was a small incident in Copiapó. You know what I'm talking about?'

Enzo doesn't hesitate; he doesn't know how to. 'That was me. The little shit would have talked.'

'Good. You did the right thing. And you got lucky. King met that boy, bought some food off him. I guess he was quite fond of him. Anyway, he's angry. You'll see him soon.'

Enzo smiles, too. 'Good.' After a beat, he adds, 'I will not let you down.'

'I don't expect you to. There's considerable rewards in it for you if you keep your word.'

'I've got to go,' Enzo says, and hangs up, his blood simmering with excitement.

For two reasons.

One: he relishes challenges. He hopes King is actually skilled, not just another weak hype-job.

Two: he hasn't killed an American in years. He deeply misses the sensation of seeing the life bleed from their eyes. He's never told anyone why he likes to make Americans hurt. The truth is, it's cathartic. He blames Operation Condor for making his father a monster, and he blames his father for … well, that's a can of worms he'd rather not crack open. Because of his old man, all Enzo knows is inflicting pain. It's his whole world. But somewhere deep below the surface, there's a dash of humanity left in him, and this microscopic part of himself *knows* he's a horrible, sadistic, cruel, unforgivable piece of filth.

It was America that made the pipe-dream of Operation Condor a reality.

It was America that created *him* and all his fucked-up behaviours.

If the United States didn't exist, maybe he'd be a normal man with a normal job. He might even have a family. It seems so ridiculous now, but he knows it's the way his life could have gone. Instead he's here, letting his most loyal soldiers develop potentially fatal altitude symptoms for no other reason than he likes it when people hurt.

So whenever he gets his hands on a "good ol' boy," he has a field day with them, makes them scream in ways they didn't think they could. It stokes some strange sense of revenge in him.

Payback for making him what he is.

He strides to the nearest tent and slaps on the canvas. 'Get up! We're moving.'

His men crawl painfully out.

36

King barely considers strategy.

Only a handful of times in his life has he been this furious. On each of the occasional times he's lost control of his emotions, he's left a sea of devastation in his wake. He knows, without a shadow of a doubt, that it will be the same here. On the long and winding drive up Ruta 31 into the foothills of the Andes, he descends into what Lars once labelled "berserker mode," unable to think of anything but the soon-to-be eviscerated bodies of the remaining soldiers.

David's smiling face is imprinted in his mind.

He knows it will stay imprinted until every last one of them is dead.

And even then, it will plague his dreams for years to come. Another horrific tragedy added to his nightmares. He knows there are other solo operators out there — the rest of the highly secretive Black Force — and he wonders if they're haunted by what they've seen, the same way he is. He hopes to one day defy protocol and meet one of his faceless peers.

Wouldn't that be something?

For now, it's a pipe dream, and he lets the hunt consume him.

Not that it's much of a "hunt," so to speak. If he cared about ingenious tactics or even his own wellbeing, he'd pull over right now, in this endless, lawless no-man's-land of a desert, and burrow down in a concealed position on one of the hills that overlook the winding road. He could camp for days on end if that's what it took, never taking his eyes off the asphalt far below. When what remained of the Argentine squad finally passed by, he'd be able to take out a couple of them at long-range — the drivers, at the very least — and once their vehicles careened off the road, the rest would be sitting ducks.

But that's not what he wants.

He wants it finished.

So as the sun continues to rise overhead, King mashes the accelerator for hours on end until he hits the Andes. He feels no fatigue and refuses to pull over to eat or drink, instead downing water and chomping through MREs as he keeps one hand on the wheel. He only makes one stop to empty his bladder — meaning that he's only spent a couple of minutes stationary all morning — and as a result he reaches the mountains before the sun hits its apex in the sky.

He recognises familiar terrain: the edge of Nevado Tres Cruces National Park.

On his right lies Salar de Maricunga, the high-altitude salt lake Friesen pointed out on their first drive in. On his left are vast plains, and beyond them, the sharp rise of snow-capped hills. The road itself is endless and shimmering. He pushes the Hilux faster, and although it groans in protest, the old truck surges faster.

From here it's a steady climb all the way up to Ojos del Salado.

He's prepared to return to twenty thousand feet.

Then a vibrating speck appears on the horizon.

At first, he thinks it's a mirage, a trick of the eye after so long spent focusing on the glare. But as he barrels toward it, the speck becomes a larger dot, which morphs into the clear outline of an off-road vehicle. The four-wheel-drive speeds north as he surges south. With no other roads or trails out here, the two parties are set to blow past each other in less than sixty seconds.

King reaches over the centre console for his duffel and unzips the long bag attached to the pack. He extracts the old-school semi-auto FN FAL that will no doubt kick like a mule. It's not quite an M16A4 with an ACOG sight, but that beautiful piece of tech was lost to the mountains, so this Cold War throwback will have to do.

Even though the oncoming 4WD is most likely civilian, he prepares for a shootout regardless.

The vehicles roar closer toward each other, and King sees two things at once.

First: it's not a false alarm; it's real. Even from a significant distance, he can make out the shape of the silhouettes in the front seats of the approaching truck. Their profiles are even wider than if they were bodybuilders, which means they're clad in combat gear, and that tells him all he needs to know.

Second: a shootout isn't the play. There simply isn't any cover he can use besides the Hilux itself, and if the approaching truck is packed with all the half-dozen remaining men, they'll be able to chew the Toyota to pieces if he pulls over and cowers behind it.

So he changes his plan.

Instead of lifting the FN FAL above the dashboard and firing the first shot of the gunfight, he keeps the rifle where it is.

He pretends he doesn't notice the armour-clad soldiers through the windshield.

The vehicles scream closer to each other.

He sees the driver assess the Hilux and instinctively disregard it. Then the man's gaze snaps over in a double-take as he identifies King through the grimy windshield. King feigns like he just noticed, too, and he widens his eyes as he wrenches his own wheel to the left.

The Hilux veers off Ruta 31 and onto the desert plain.

King speeds for the distant hills.

Behind him, the carful of soldiers follows in hot pursuit. They think they've caught him off-guard. He imagines them chomping at the bit, ecstatic at how it all unfolded.

Better not prove them right, he thinks as he surveys the hills that he speeds towards. Before he lurched off-road, he concocted another mad idea, unsure if it was even feasible.

Now he has no choice but to try it.

37

'Got him,' Enzo whispers from the rear middle seat, one gloved hand on each of the front seat backs.

He cranes his neck to get the best possible look at the Toyota Hilux as they speed after it. Bautista, his man behind the wheel, is in bad shape from the altitude, but that doesn't matter. On their way down from Ojos del Salado, Enzo pictured a hundred different versions of what might happen when they ran into the American. Catching him completely by surprise was perhaps the best-case scenario, and now they're living it.

Sometimes fate is kind.

Jason King, Enzo thinks, rolling the name through his mind. West hinted at King's fearsome reputation, and Enzo figures he'll keep the man's head.

Hunched over the wheel as he thrashes the accelerator, Bautista spits, '*¿Adónde diablos va?*'

Where the hell is he going?

'Good question,' Enzo says, the whole SUV rattling

around them. They're doing more than ninety miles an hour across the desert flat.

Ahead lies nothing but the severe slopes of snow-capped hills. The Hilux barrels toward the steepest incline, and with a burst of extra acceleration, mounts it. Enzo watches the chassis shudder, and loose rocks spew from underneath the vehicle. Engine screaming, audible even over the sound of their own, King's truck begins to climb.

'A game of chicken,' Bautista says in Spanish. 'He wants us to play.'

Enzo smiles. 'Then let's play.'

The passenger, a competent soldier named Tomas, says, 'Shouldn't we just wait for him to—?'

Enzo brings his trusted Makarov pistol up to the side of the man's head and pulls the trigger.

Gore showers the passenger window.

Bautista's eyes widen; the two men in the back with Enzo turn statuesque. Suddenly manic, Enzo grips the driver by the back of the neck and screams in his ear: '*Do you want to wait, too?!*'

'*No!*' Bautista roars back. '*No, I don't!*'

'*Then get the fuck up there!*'

Bautista hadn't even slowed, but Enzo now knows there's no chance he'll touch the brake. In truth, Tomas had it coming: the execution served a purpose besides simple shock-and-awe. For months, Enzo watched doubt creep into the young and talented soldier's mindset until, before they knew it, the kid was questioning every choice his commander made. If hesitation exists in your mind, all the natural ability in the world means nothing, and Enzo had already decided that Tomas was done as an elite soldier in his unit. It was a simple coincidence that the opportunity to use him as an example arose.

There isn't a chance in hell that the surviving three will disobey him.

Sure enough, Bautista guns it up the hillside without hesitation, throwing them all back in their seats.

Enzo wears a grin as the back of his skull lashes the headrest behind.

He smiles because he knows that King can't win a game of chicken against Bautista. The man knows that touching the brake will be met with a bullet, and he'd rather die brave than a coward.

Jason King's death is inevitable.

The world outside the windows goes diagonal as the gradient steepens.

Enzo's stomach drops, and he reloads his Makarov despite only firing one round. Something tells him he may need a full clip.

Then he holds on for the ride.

38

They're brave.

King has to give them that.

He feared they might bail before he could bring his mad idea to fruition, but the pursuing four-wheel-drive follows him doggedly up the hill. His internal organs do cartwheels as he pushes the Hilux up steeper and steeper terrain; gravity pins him to the driver's seat. At any moment he expects to feel the tyres skid out beneath him, and he forces himself to stay constantly ready for an unexpected barrel-roll.

By this point, he's not sure it would be survivable.

Life-or-death urgency lends him pure focus.

Dead ahead (or, rather, *above*), he spots what he's looking for. The hill he's climbing tops out against the base of a sheer rock wall, its craggy features coated in a thin layer of sand and dust. Further up, the rock wall becomes another, larger hill, but there's no way to access the higher ground by vehicle. King accelerates toward the wall instead of searching for a path around it. The surrounding terrain lends believability to his performance — there might be a way up, but it's so precarious that it doesn't seem suspicious for him not to veer left or right.

Below, the Argentines must think he's passed the point of no return. He can't bring the Hilux to a stop, or the tyres might lose traction on the dust. He can't turn to bail out of the ascent, or he might lose the fight with gravity and send the car barrel-rolling down the slope.

He surges closer to the wall, squinting to make out the point where the hillside meets the rock.

He thanks his lucky stars.

It's not a hard right-angle; the dirt concentrated around the base of the wall forms a gentle curve, like a naturally-formed ramp. If he accelerates into it, at least he won't squash the Hilux into the wall like crushing a can. What happens beyond that is anyone's guess, but he thinks that maybe, just *maybe,* he can pull this off.

He locks his gaze on the rearview mirror.

The Argentines' off-road truck, far more expensive than the battered Toyota, is gaining ground. King watches as the four-wheel-drive with its modified suspension tackles the slope effortlessly. It powers up into range, and a figure clad all in black leans out the rear passenger window with another FN FAL in a double-handed grip. King's vision is blurred from the Hilux rattling all around him, but he makes out one identifiable feature: the grizzled soldier wears an eyepatch.

In a flash, the man takes aim and fires.

King ducks at precisely the right moment. As the rear windshield shatters and the headrest above and behind him explodes in a shower of foam, he realises the man is a fright-eningly good shot. King doubts even *he* could hit a target in those circumstances: one moving vehicle to another, both of them shaking and bouncing up the terrain. He only hit his targets from Friesen's jeep yesterday because they were stationary.

So even if he wanted to bail on this suicidal plan, he now has no choice.

Another couple of seconds and the Argentine will smoke him like a pin cushion.

He takes a risk, sits up, and assesses the trajectory.

It'll be close.

But it's his only option, so he goes for it. All he has to do is aim for the rock wall and not take his foot off the accelerator. Still, it scares the living shit out of him. Every impulse urges him to lift his boot, but he doesn't.

At the last second, he grabs the FAL, pops the driver's door, and pushes out of the cabin.

He timed it perfectly; he had to. Half a second earlier and the Hilux wouldn't have enough momentum to shoot up the dirt ramp. Half a second later and he'd have been trapped inside for what came next...

As he falls from the vehicle, it speeds away from him, fast enough for the door frame to clip his ankles on the way out. He spins wildly in the air, legs flailing, and comes down in a violent heap on the hillside. The impact aggravates all the soft tissue damage he sustained the day before. His shoulders and hips scream as he skids in the dust.

But he lands on his back, offering him a view of the Hilux's trajectory.

Its front tyres mount the natural ramp and its engine roars as the hood lifts towards the sky. The tyres find purchase on the rock wall itself, but not before shearing a chunk of the hood off in a scream of metal and sparks. The pickup seems to hang in the air for a strange moment, completely vertical.

Then gravity does its job.

The vehicle has just enough momentum for the rear tyres to hit the dirt ramp, and it hits the tipping point.

The hood pitches backwards, away from the wall, with a colossal groan.

The equivalent of a backwards somersault, nose over tail.

The rest is inevitable. The Hilux falls back on its roof, blowing out all the glass. Anyone still inside would have been squashed like a bug. Instead of coming to rest, the vehicle flips again, sending debris flying. At that point, King knows for sure that there's no stopping its descent, and he cranes his neck to get a look at its path.

The Argentines' truck has nowhere to go.

Its driver sees what's happening and slams the brakes, but it achieves nothing. The Hilux crashes and tumbles down the hillside, turning end over end in a straight line.

The soldier with the FAL, still leaning out the open window, sees it coming. He has a split second to save himself, and he does. He kicks off the seat he's perched on, and throws himself headfirst out of the truck.

Just in time.

Four thousand pounds of metal crashes into the Argentines' vehicle like a falling boulder.

39

There's no chance of survival for whoever's still inside the metal tomb.

The wreckage of the Hilux, along with the squashed remnants of its target, spin and tumble their way down the hillside, both of which shed debris with each revolution. Shards of glass fly everywhere, and twisted hunks of chassis rip off the mechanical carcasses.

In seconds, both vehicles are hundreds of feet down the slope.

All at once, it's eerily quiet.

Just a soft desert wind whistling over the plains.

King planned for significant injuries, and after the way he landed, there's no way he isn't badly hurt. But as he struggles to his feet, he refuses to take stock.

The soldier who hurled himself out of the window is alive, positioned on all fours a couple of dozen feet downhill.

King finds it hard to put any weight on his left leg, and the nauseating sensation suggests that a ligament is torn — maybe even his ACL. If so, the recovery will be long and brutal, but he can't worry about that now: he still needs to make it out of this alive.

If his plan worked — which it did — he hadn't expected anyone to survive.

But the guy with the eyepatch has dogged determination. He must have landed just as hard, but he struggles to his feet like King. Both panting for breath, they face each other on the slope. King stares down from the high ground: not that it means much.

They both leapt out of their respective trucks clutching FN FALs.

Both rifles are nowhere to be seen, lost in the carnage.

King doesn't bother looking around for his. He darts a hand for his abdomen holster and rips out the SIG Sauer P226 resting within. But the Argentine had exactly the same idea, and both men draw their pistols in unison.

Like some twisted mirror image of a Wild West gunslinger duel.

With his SIG halfway up, King reflects on the soldier's scary accuracy with the FAL and knows the inevitable outcome. They'll shoot at the same time, hit each other at the same time. They'll both die in this desert. And he isn't willing to sacrifice himself to kill this man. He's got a lot of living left to do.

So he bails on the quickdraw and throws himself behind a low boulder to his left, flattening himself into the dust.

The Argentine fires twice.

Hits rock.

King springs up, draws a bead, and triple-taps the trigger.

His shots hit empty air. There's no shortage of natural cover on the craggy slope, and the soldier hurled himself behind a similar formation. King catches a sliver of his profile and triple-taps again.

Nothing lands.

In the blink of an eye, the Argentine comes back with another pair of bullets. King feels the displaced air of the second shot; every muscle in his body tenses involuntarily. He musters his courage and simply inches to the left. In the heat of the moment, his enemy won't notice the imperceptible movement, and when he believes that King hasn't moved, he'll impulsively fire at the same point in space.

He does.

Misses again with another double-tap.

King fires three times again, but he's never seen a hostile move so fast. Still, the three-round bursts finally pay off. Although the soldier disappears behind cover with the speed of a panther, the third bullet grazes the side of his head. King doesn't see it, but he hears the uncontrollable scream and knows what must have happened.

The Argentine panics.

The pain makes him desperate, and he lurches up and fires another pair of shots.

King got greedy. He thought he had it in the bag; the immediate retaliation caught him off-guard.

He takes both shots in the chest.

The Kevlar saves him, but it's like taking a battering ram to the heart. His boots skid on the dust and he sends loose dirt flying as he falls back, the breath smashed out of him. Suspended in the air, he realises this may be his best chance, and he risks it all.

Going down, he fires his last three rounds at the Argentine's exposed profile.

His spare twelve-round mags of .40 S&W are in his duffel, buried in the Hilux.

This is it.

He falls behind the boulder, losing his line of sight, so there's no way to tell whether he struck home or not. Winded, exhausted, beat to shit, lacking the use of his left leg, he drags himself to a seated position and crawls to the edge of the big rock. He takes a careful look around the side.

No sign of his enemy.

The hills are quiet; only the piercing whine of tinnitus in his ears.

He coughs blood, but refuses to take his eyes off the rock formation below.

Then, like something from the abyss, the soldier rises from behind one of the boulders.

40

The guy's in bad shape.

But alive.

The shot that grazed the side of his head didn't just carve a line through his flesh: it ripped his eyepatch off. Blood pools in the shrunken socket. The left half of his face is crimson. The gunk flows in rivulets down his cheek, dripping off his chin. Each time he exhales, he spits a cloud of the stuff.

Still, none of the final three shots struck home.

Now King's a sitting duck.

He gets ready to retreat behind the boulder and fall back on pure desperation. He doesn't know what he'll do. A small voice in the back of his head tells him this is the end.

Then the panting soldier holds up his sidearm, as if presenting it to King.

King identifies the weapon: an old Makarov, almost certainly sporting the standard eight-round detachable box magazine. He knows the Argentine fired four double-taps. He can barely believe his good fortune.

It gets stranger, even more surreal, when the hostile actually calls out to him in accented English. 'You out?'

King drags himself shakily to his feet. He isn't sure why he's interacting.

Maybe some subtle sense of honour, whatever that may be.

He holds up his own SIG. 'I had twelve.'

The bleeding soldier pauses for thought. 'You've used twelve.'

'Uh-huh.'

Silence. King's in tremendous agony, and knows his enemy must be, too. Perhaps that's why they're doing this. They're both in heightened states, riding that fine line, each of them clinging to consciousness.

'You got spares?' the soldier shouts.

'No.'

'You lying?'

King doesn't respond.

The Argentine takes a final look at his Makarov, as if its empty magazine might regenerate bullets.

Then he sighs and tosses it.

'If you're lying,' the Argentine shouts, 'you win.'

King throws his SIG away in turn.

The soldier watches it happen with mounting disbelief before his surprise gives way to bemusement. He chuckles wryly, rolling his shoulders in their sockets. 'Maybe this was meant to be.'

'You see your rifle?' King shouts down.

The soldier looks all around. 'No luck. You?'

King glances left, then right. Nothing but craggy hillside. 'Me neither.'

'You going to come down here?' The guy has to catch his

breath between sentences; he's hurting. 'Or should I come up there?'

King considers the odds that this soldier is the culprit, the target of all his rage. *One in ten, or thereabouts.* He isn't exactly sure how many men he just crushed to death; he knows he killed five yesterday.

'You should walk away,' he calls out. 'If it was one of your buddies who killed that boy in Copiapó, then leave. Whoever it was, they've paid the price. As for trying to take me out ... you were just following orders — I get it.' He knows his mercy might be mistaken for weakness, but he doesn't care. He presses on. 'Tell me you didn't lay your hands on David, and then walk.'

His logic is flawed, no doubt. This guy might well have done it, and if he did, he won't admit it. He'll take the opportunity and bounce. King will never know who was truly guilty.

Then the one-eyed man smiles. There's no humour in the expression. It's sardonic, bitter.

Instantly King knows the truth.

Then the soldier confirms it.

'I choked the little guy to death,' he spits. The wind carries his words up the slope. 'I watched the life go from his eyes. You know what? I wish you knew him better. I wish it hurt you *more.* You might kill me, but you'll never get him back.'

All the injuries and fatigue wash away in an instant, replaced by dark fury. Blood roars in King's ears as his vision shrinks to a tunnel, with the Argentine square in the metaphorical crosshairs.

'And I would never walk away,' the soldier yells, 'even if I didn't kill that brat. Because you are an American. You could offer me a billion and I wouldn't walk away.'

King's legs take on a life of their own. He forgets that his knee is blown out, ignores it entirely, and slowly strides down the hillside toward the man.

The soldier isn't fazed. He stands there, watching keenly, practically salivating.

Waiting to pounce.

King doesn't have to shout anymore; the soldier's well within earshot. 'Americans did that to your eye, I take it?'

He looks the big man up and down for the first time, and notices he's missing a finger, too.

The soldier grins through bloody teeth. 'In a round-about way … yeah.'

King grinds to a halt, ten paces from making contact.

The soldier watches his every move, his sole pupil dilated.

'Jason King,' the man purrs.

King's heart lurches. 'Who sent you?'

The soldier shakes his head.

'Do I know you?' King asks.

'I doubt it. I am Enzo Navarro.'

'Never heard of you.'

Enzo smiles. 'That's good. I like to hear that. Now, there is the matter of that young child. You must avenge him.'

He stands there, expecting the bullrush.

King knows he needs to get under the man's skin. They're equally damaged and compromised, so it's going to come down to emotional control. Whoever makes the first impulsive mistake is going to lose.

King forces the image of David out of his mind, tries to forget the kid exists.

He points to Enzo's shrivelled eye socket. 'In a round-about way, you said?'

'My father,' Enzo replies, stone-faced. 'He made me what I am. The Americans made *him* what he was.'

King makes calculations — what involvement would the U.S. have had with an Argentine man roughly thirty years Enzo's senior? The most obvious answer is the most likely.

'Condor?' he asks.

Enzo doesn't speak, but anger flares in his eye, which gives King his answer. He can see the soldier nearly lost control, almost charged at him just for namedropping the operation.

He knows he has to tip Enzo over the edge.

Personally, he thinks that Operation Condor — the South American campaign of oppression and terror backed by America in the seventies — was despicable, if not pure evil, but Enzo doesn't need to know that. The child-killer must see what he expects to see if he's going to drop his guard.

So King stomachs a strange touch of guilt, then hardens his face.

'Looks like we only half-trained your dad,' he says. 'We did a whole lot worse back then — you got off easy. He should've taken both your eyes. Should've crippled you like we crippled your soft country.'

Enzo snarls like an animal and lunges at King with murderous intent.

41

Enzo Navarro makes the age-old mistake.

King's seen it too many times to count.

Men who were born to fight, born to hunt, born to kill ... they assume their rage is the answer. Enzo's angry enough to believe it's a superpower. He sees pure red, wants to rip King limb from limb, and all caution falls by the wayside. King made sure not to make that mistake; he was furious on the drive up from Copiapó, but he knew he could tame it when it mattered.

Like right now.

Enzo ducks low and catches him around the legs and tries to drive him back into the hill. At the slightest contact, King's left knee explodes with pain, but it doesn't stop him from executing a "whizzer," a known staple of wrestling. He hooks his arm above Enzo's elbow and wrenches with all his might. The Argentine's momentum works against him as he flies sideways, catapulting away just as King's knee gives out, and they both sprawl to the earth.

In unison, they roll toward each other to try and inflict a debilitating strike.

Enzo rolls first, then throws a looping punch.

King throws a haymaker of his own *as* he's rolling.

So he lands first.

Drives his calloused knuckles into Enzo's midsection, hard enough to feel his fist squash the man's stomach. Enzo chokes on his own breath as he tries to inhale while air explodes up his windpipe.

A bystander wouldn't notice Enzo freezing up as his throat spasms — he only hesitates for milliseconds — but King sees it.

He lunges forward and slices one leg over the top of Enzo's torso, straddling his ribcage. Two hundred and twenty pounds on your midsection makes it awfully difficult to move, even with the adrenaline. Enzo bucks and lurches beneath King, but within a moment he knows he's beat, so he rolls onto his front to prevent King from raining punches and elbows down on his unprotected face.

Which only makes it worse.

He's lying facedown now, wearing his foe like a backpack, and King loops an arm around his neck from behind and locks in a vicious rear-naked choke. He feels everything he expects to feel: his forearm crushing Enzo's soft throat, the Argentine spluttering and wheezing, the sudden avalanche of blood that pours from Enzo's cut as King squeezes harder...

Enzo rolls again, and King follows him over. Now the Argentine faces the cloudless sky, King underneath him with the choke locked in tight.

He cranks harder, thinking of David.

He feels soft tissue give way under the massive pressure.

It's inevitable now: Enzo's going to die. Already the damage to his throat is irreparable, his head is turning the colour of a beetroot, the capillaries in his one good eye are starting to burst. Not to mention the blood loss...

But the Argentine suddenly understands that. At that point, some men accept their fate, and others fight with everything they have left even though they know it's futile, purely out of spite.

Enzo falls in the latter category.

He reaches back, finds King's face, and digs a gloved finger into each of his eyes.

King goes immediately blind. The pressure and the pain is so sudden, so severe, that his automatic instinct is to let go of the choke.

But he doesn't.

He holds on, because he's brutally aware that his arms are burned out. If he releases the hold to swat Enzo's hand away, he may not regain the advantage again. They're both so tired it's like they're fighting underwater, and there's no telling whose energy reserves will give out first.

But Enzo pushes his fingers deeper, groaning like a man possessed.

The sensation in King's eyeballs is horrific.

Indescribable.

A few more ounces of pressure, and he knows he may never see again.

Knows his eyeballs may well pop.

He wrenches the choke as tight as humanly possible, screaming from the exertion. He feels everything in Enzo's throat give way, and he knows he's now crushing the man's windpipe. But somehow the fingers are still in his eyes.

The bastard just *won't die*...

Enzo roars, too, and pushes even harder against King's eyelids.

Like someone's drilling into his brain, holding a flaming torch to his nerve endings...

Suddenly, King sees David's face on the blank canvas of his vision. Maybe it's his life flashing before his eyes. Whatever the case, it's real.

The little boy beams and says, *'It is the nice to meet of you!'*

A picture of beautiful innocence.

King finds something deeper and forgets the lactic acid in his muscles, forgets his pain and exhaustion and delirium, forgets the agony in his eye sockets.

He just tightens the choke until he's using an inhuman amount of strength.

As Enzo's neck flattens, the soldier gives a final, resigned splutter.

His limbs go slack, and his fingers fall away.

King throws the body off. He only hears it slap the hillside unceremoniously; he doesn't see it.

He's blind.

K	ing considers it his crowning achievement that he doesn't panic.

Most would fall to pieces thinking their sight was gone forever, even hardened killers. It would be devastating, of course: his career over in a blink, life as he knows it fundamentally altered. But after the vision of David, he'd made a decision.

Accepted his fate.

Whatever it took, he would kill the boy's murderer, even if it meant death or permanent injury.

So he sits on the hillside beside Enzo's corpse and watches the fuzzy stars dance across the blackness. He controls his breathing, fights the urge to lie back and pass out right here.

Slowly, the stars recede.

The darkness opens up.

Light ebbs in.

It takes a full fifteen minutes for his vision to return. Even then, the sweeping desert plains are blurred and fuzzy, the hills mere outlines below a brilliant blue sky. The incapacitation might last days, even weeks, but eventually he knows he will heal. He finally breathes a sigh of relief. Enzo didn't push hard enough, didn't have the strength to hold on long enough to cause permanent damage.

In some strange way, it floods King with hope.

He met pure fury head-on and won.

In truth, he doubted himself. Anger like Enzo's is terrifying to behold, even if you're one of the most dangerous men alive. Just considering what Enzo would have done to him if he was overpowered is enough nightmare fuel for the rest of King's days. Add to that the fatigue from the climb to twenty thousand feet, followed by the mad descent, and King honestly questioned whether he had a chance.

Enzo was good.

One of the best.

But all of that falls away when King realises the most important thing.

He knew my name.

43

W hen the Globemaster lands and the rear ramp descends, Allan Friesen doesn't see the Homestead Air Reserve Base in Florida.

Instead, he looks out across the tarmac and recognises the place.

Andrews Air Force Base, only a few miles from Washington D.C.

Shit, he thinks.

He gathers up his gear and heads slowly down the ramp as a black Suburban pulls up on the runway below. He takes his time, placing his boots carefully on the metal, one deliberate step after the other. He's in no rush. He knows he should be savouring each breath. When he steps down on the tarmac, he tries the passenger door. It's unlocked, but he only gets it open a few inches before someone inside yanks it closed, tearing the handle from his grasp. The windows are so tinted that he didn't know someone was sitting on the other side of the glass.

He pulls the rear passenger door instead, and slides in across a row of empty seats.

The driver's an ordinary guy wearing a shapeless white open-collared shirt. From behind, Friesen can only see the passenger's back, but he gets the picture. The hulking man, clad in body armour, wears a thick black balaclava to obscure his features. When he twists in his seat to face Friesen, it reveals the white skull spray-painted on the wool. The guy's wide, unblinking eyes are the only skin visible beneath all the gear.

'You gonna be a problem?' the passenger asks.

Wait, Friesen realises. *That's not him.*

It's subtle, barely noticeable, but the voice has the slight distortion of being projected through a speaker. There must be a device embedded under the mask. Friesen thought he'd seen it all, but this is strangely eerie.

In response, he stares blankly at the skull mask. He's been a spook for years. Nothing's going to outwardly deter him. 'If I wanted to be a problem, I'd never have come back.'

'But you did,' the tinny voice says. 'Because you know your place.'

'Mmm.'

With a flash of movement, the skull mask faces forward, and the driver puts the Suburban in gear and peels off the runway. Friesen sits back and closes his eyes. It doesn't matter where they're going, and he refrains from memorising their route. He didn't waltz back into the hands of the people whose plans he disrupted just to plan a hair-raising breakout. If he wanted to run, he'd have run: exactly what he told the brute up front.

Who that brute serves as a mouthpiece for is anyone's guess.

Friesen's sure he'll find out.

Their journey lasts twenty-six minutes. He tries not to keep track of time, but by now it's an automatic habit. The driver pulls to a stop and unbuckles his seatbelt; the *click* makes Friesen open his eyes. They're parked in a loading bay, the walls and floor and ceiling all impenetrable concrete.

It feels like he's already in prison.

At least it's not an overseas black site: he's visited his fair share of *those* prisons, and he's just grateful not to be on the other side of the bars in a hellhole like that.

He steps out of the vehicle and the brute in the skull mask gives him a thorough pat-down, stripping him of anything that might constitute a weapon. Relieved of almost every possession on his person, Friesen lets the enforcer lead him deep into the building and shepherd him into a private elevator. The brute leans into the cable car, taps one of the two buttons on the panel, then steps out. The doors whisper closed; as they shut, the skull leers, until finally they meet in the middle of the balaclava and the enforcer disappears from sight.

Friesen's alone.

He takes long, deep breaths as the elevator ascends. Hard to keep the claustrophobia at bay. He's faced danger so many times he thought he was numb to it, but this is a different beast. It's so quiet. He's used to explosions and screaming and hellfire.

When the doors open again, Friesen comes face-to-face with a tall man in his fifties sporting a mane of long black hair. The stranger is unarmed, and above all else, it's that detail which shocks Friesen to his core. The guy isn't a combatant: he's big, heavily muscled, but it's commercial fitness, not functional power. Nevertheless, he exudes a confidence Friesen has seldom witnessed. It's like he owns not just the room, but the whole building, even the city at large.

Maybe he does, Friesen thinks.

'You're not Lars,' he says.

'That's right,' the man says. 'I sent Lars home a few hours ago.'

Which conveys everything about the sort of power the guy wields.

Nobody tells Lars Crawford what to do: *nobody.*

Except maybe one man.

'My name is Christian West,' he says. 'That won't mean anything to you. But I'd wager you've heard a couple of passing references to an authority known as "The Golden One."'

Allan Friesen, who's seen all the horrors that humanity has to offer, suddenly wilts. All at once he understands the gravity of where he is and who he's speaking with. He also understands that you don't get shown the very top of the pyramid if you're allowed to live to speak about it.

He's a dead man walking.

His fate is sealed.

Pulse pounding, he steps out of the elevator and walks right up to Christian West. They're mere feet apart: Friesen, and the man who runs the country.

Voice low, Friesen says, 'I could kill you before they get to me.'

'You probably could,' West says with a charismatic smile. 'But you won't.'

He turns on his heel and leads Friesen down a long corridor, through an antechamber, and into a sweeping office that overlooks the city. Friesen isn't sure why he follows, why he obeys.

He just does.

44

"The Golden One" crosses to a giant desk and takes a seat behind it.

Friesen stands in front of the walnut slab, as if at attention. No one orders him to. There isn't a physical threat. Only an implied one.

But he complies all the same.

West tilts his chair back and interlocks his hands behind his head. He lets out a quiet sigh. 'You knew what we were planning.'

Friesen swallows. 'Lars said nothing about—'

'Obviously Lars told you nothing. But still, you knew.'

Friesen didn't come back voluntarily just to bullshit. 'Yeah.'

'You could've stayed out of the way.'

'Yeah.'

'King was compromised. He didn't know you had a backup vehicle. He'd never have found it on his own. Up against an elite hit squad headed by Enzo Navarro, it wouldn't have been much of a contest. He'd have lost, and you could have walked away.'

Friesen barely hesitates. 'Yeah.'

'Knowing all this, you came back to us. You didn't cut your losses and run.'

'Yeah.'

West purses his lips, ruminating. 'Do you expect me to be impressed?'

'I don't expect anything. I don't know you.'

'I'm not impressed,' West goes on, as if Friesen hadn't spoken at all. 'I think selflessness is the stupidest fucking thing on the planet. What exactly do you think you're achieving?'

'I'm doing what I think is right.'

'You're an idiot.'

Friesen shrugs.

Antsy, West sits forward in the chair and scratches at his stubble. 'The problem is, Allan, that I've changed my mind. The war against Jason King is over. I'm putting him back to work.'

'What?'

'Weren't expecting that, huh? You heard me. From the moment I made the decision to dissolve Black Force, I was like a rabid dog frothing at the mouth to get the job done. But as things unfolded ... well, the way they unfolded — I couldn't see what was right in front of me. I didn't detach, didn't take a step back and analyse the situation, and that's the most important part of what we do, isn't it?'

Friesen doesn't answer.

'You know it is,' West goes on. 'I should have been objective about how King took out the first half of Enzo's squad. That's not to say your driving wasn't impressive, but the way King tore through those men ... it was otherworldly. For some reason, I thought Enzo was different. Thought it would *be* different. Now here we are.' He pauses for thought.

'At least this little expedition showed me the quality of the division I was trying to eradicate. I just need to utilise them better, *smarter.*'

Friesen wonders why West is bothering telling him any of this.

Then it clicks.

'You want me to reach out to King,' he says, voicing his realisation. 'You want me to tell him it wasn't the betrayal we thought it was, that he's clear to come back into the fold. That he's not in danger from his own countrymen. That it was something else, some geopolitical mystery. A giant fuck-up, but nothing malicious on Uncle Sam's end.'

West's blue eyes light up as he nods. 'You're good, Allan.'

Friesen stares. 'You're about to tell me I'll be rewarded for making this call. The reward will be my life. If I refuse, you'll kill me.'

West slowly nods.

'You'll be lying,' Friesen says suddenly. It's confrontational, and he doesn't shy away from it. 'Really, you're going to kill me either way, and you're hoping that I don't realise. But I do.'

West visibly stiffens. Instinctively, he raises his right hand from beneath the desk, revealing a Desert Eagle clutched tight. The angles and distances don't favour Friesen. If he tries lunging across the walnut slab, even an incompetent marksman could turn his head into a crater before he got his hands on them.

Softly, West says, 'You're *very* good, Allan. You see things the way they are, not the way you wish they were. That's a rare trait.' He sighs. It's a shame...' He trails off, all but confirming Friesen's accusation.

Friesen knows this is the part where he might waver. He steeled himself for this, knew it was coming well in advance, but he figured it was better to die cleanly here in this thickly-carpeted office than to be hunted through foreign lands for the rest of his days.

But he's aware that we usually know what's right: we just don't do it.

He should stand tall and hold his head high, and he tries to, but he finds himself fighting a wave of sudden existential dread.

Then he pulls himself together anyway, and corrects his posture.

Voice neutral, he says, 'If I refuse to make the call, what happens?'

'I shoot you where you're standing. King gets spooked from the radio silence and never comes back to us. I'm forced to dedicate a tremendous amount of resources to tracking him down and neutralising him. I can't afford not to, given all that juicy knowledge in his head. Sure, wave after wave of my men will die — as Ojos del Salado proved — but I'll eventually wear him down and finish it. You know I will, or you'd already have refused. And I'd very much like to avoid that outcome. I genuinely want him back so we can move past this business and get him back to work.'

'And if I make the call?'

'He won't be in danger. I no longer stand to gain anything from his death. You can see that now. I wasn't paying enough attention — he's better than I thought he was. I want to use him for five or ten more years, and if he makes it out the other side, I'll let him walk free. You have my word.'

'Why would I ever trust your word?'

'You can't. Not unequivocally. But if you're smart, you'll see that making the call is your only option. Refusing guarantees King's death. Not today, but eventually. I won't ever stop hunting him.'

'He's better than you thought,' Friesen repeats back to West. 'You might never get him.'

'That's your call. It's your choice. It needs to be voluntary, or King will sense something's up.'

West tosses a sat phone.

Friesen catches it, and for a long, drawn-out minute, he gazes down at its black screen.

He makes his decision.

45

The sat phone rings in its pouch on King's belt.

An unknown number, but there's only one person it could be.

Sitting in the dust, leaning back against the hillside, he gazes out over the desert. He killed Enzo more than an hour ago, and still he hasn't moved. Like wet concrete solidifying, his muscles lock in place every time he makes minor adjustments to his position. He's beyond fatigue, way out in uncharted waters. His vision is no better; the world's still bleary.

But he can lift the phone to his ear and answer. He can do that much.

Allan Friesen deserves it.

'You made it?' he asks after struggling through the movement.

'I made it,' Friesen says, voice unreadable. 'It wasn't them.'

It jolts King, and he sits up a little straighter. 'Are you sure?'

'One hundred percent.'

'Are they making you say this?'

'Nah.'

King's stomach drops, and his blood runs cold. Friesen's telling the truth. On the drive back to Copiapó, they decided on a simple verbal tripwire: if King asked such a question and Friesen responded with, '*No,*' it meant he was under duress. Any variation of the word — '*nup,*' '*nada,*' '*nah*' — meant it was clear.

'Shit,' King says finally. His head spins. 'Then who the fuck was it?'

'Your guess is as good as mine. I don't have any more intel — nothing useful, anyway. But they're reeling. They're digging deep into the history of Reece Evans. No telling whether they'll get to the bottom of it, but the vetting process is sure getting an overhaul. Lars thinks you'll never trust him again. He's tearing his hair out.'

'He should be. Even if it wasn't them, it wouldn't have happened if we were competent.'

'I know. Lars knows. I'm sure you'll get the mother of all apologies in-person.'

King sighs, rubs his chin. 'What's in store for you now?'

'Back to the CIA. I'm told they already miss me at SAC.'

King scrutinises Friesen's voice for any hint of deception. He doesn't detect anything. It could be a case of the spook being an excellent liar — in his line of work, you have to be — but no alarm bells go off.

Still, he has to check. 'You're not being punished?'

'Not as far as I know.'

'Do they know you had a backup plan because you suspected they'd betray you?'

'Yeah, they know.'

'What'd they think of that decision?'

'They called me paranoid. That's about it.'

'"About"?'

'Listen,' Friesen says. 'It's not your problem. Maybe I'll get a slap on the wrist. What's it matter?'

'You're right.' King sighs. 'So you're signing off?'

'It was a fun detour, I'll give you that. But it's about time I got back to my actual job. What about you? Still laying low?'

'Uh…' King trails off, gazing down at the fuzzy outline of the two-vehicle pile-up at the bottom of the hill. Then he looks over at the blur of Enzo's broken body. 'Not exactly.'

'Shit. They found you?'

King says nothing.

'Jason…?'

'I found them.'

A long silence. 'You went back?'

'They killed the boy who served us *pan con chicharrón*. His mother, too. I assume because Reece told the kid I was a soldier. And lucky I went back for the rest — the last survivor ended up being the one who did it. They're all gone now. Not that that means anything…'

Friesen doesn't respond. How can he? What would suffice? David was eight, nine years old. Not even crushing the life out of Enzo Navarro had done anything to remedy the tragedy; what use were words?

Eventually, though, Friesen says, 'I wish I tried one of those sandwiches. I was too busy second-guessing everyone. Didn't stop and appreciate the small moments.' He hesitates. 'You know, now that I think about it, I never appreciated much. Too busy…'

It sounds awfully like he's reminiscing on his life, expecting it not to last much longer. *Still paranoid*, King thinks.

'Don't talk like that,' King says. 'You got a lot of years left yet.'

'Yeah.'

'Hit me up for a beer sometime.'

'Yeah, maybe,' Friesen says, noncommittal.

With that, King knows the spook has been ordered to never contact him again. It's standard procedure, and he doesn't blame the man. The gravity of their work demands that they be professionals.

'Thanks for everything, brother,' King says. 'You saved my life. I hope you know that.'

'Just doing what's right.'

Friesen hangs up.

King puts the phone down, knowing they'll never speak again.

46

F riesen hits END CALL.

He lowers the phone, exhales, and closes his eyes.

Just doing what's right.

It's all he's ever done.

He's proud of himself, and he believes that genuine self-pride is the key to a life-well lived. You can keep secrets from whoever you want, but you sure can't hide from yourself. He knows that when Christian West reaches the end of his life, no matter how much the titan tries to convince himself otherwise, he won't feel that same pride.

That's enough for Friesen to find peace.

At the last moment, he remembers what King said about Evans, and opens his eyes. 'Why Reece?'

West, who's been keenly watching, blinks. 'What do you mean?'

'Why an untrained mountain climber?'

'Anyone competent on our side wouldn't have done it,' West admits. 'They'd have carried too much respect for King. Like you.'

Because King is a good man, Friesen thinks.

He's proud of what he did.

There's a half-smile on his face as the .50 Action Express round punches through his skull.

47

Five days later...

King meets the same Globemaster at *Aeropuerto Copiapó.*

On a chilly grey evening, as wind howls over the surrounding desert flats, he hunches against the gusts and watches the aft ramp lower with 20/20 vision.

His eyes healed faster than he expected.

The rest of him took longer, and he's not out of the woods yet. Some physical efforts permanently change you, and King feels altered at a deeper level. He knows much of that will recede as his central nervous system recovers, but not all. He broke through barriers in his mind in South America. He's leaving with a better understanding of what he's capable of, but far less of an understanding than ever of what his superiors are up to. He believes what Friesen told him, but not fully.

There are things he will never know, confirmations he will never receive, and he has to accept that.

He had a choice between going back and walking away

forever. He spent much of the last five days making that decision while he worked his way painstakingly back to Copiapó. After the call with Friesen, it took him nearly an hour to make his way down the slope and wrestle his duffel out of the Hilux's wreckage. Then there was the slog of hitching rides from suspicious Chileans, one after the other. Some were happy to drive him for free, some demanded money. The forty grand he had left in the bottom of his pack helped with that. Before each ride, he tucked away anything resembling military gear, put on his best poker face, and adopted the role of a moronic American who'd chosen to hike solo and bitten off far more than they could chew. It at least explained his state of pure exhaustion.

He made it to Copiapó, holed up in the shipping container again, and lay low for four days while considering his future.

The owner of the gas station never showed his face.

Too ashamed, probably.

Now King strides up into the cargo compartment, still wondering if he's making the right call. If he isn't, he won't know until it's too late, which makes it a little easier to accept.

It's out of his hands.

He drops down on one of the metal seats and sits straight-backed. The pilots and the loadmaster — all fresh faces — treat him like he's radioactive, as if making eye contact will hurt them. King doesn't mind. The deniable side of military operations comes with all sorts of strange caveats.

Then, moments before takeoff, the loadmaster walks over to King and wordlessly hands him a brand-new satellite phone. A glance at the screen reveals an international call is live.

King sighs and takes the phone as the loadmaster retreats. He presses it to his ear, a touch apprehensively. 'What?'

Lars Crawford says, 'I thought we'd never hear from you again.'

It's the first time they've spoken since he first touched down in Chile.

King says, 'Sorry to disappoint you.'

'I promise you we're taking every action to—'

'Lars?'

'Yes?'

'I don't care.'

Silence.

'It's your fuck-up,' King says. 'Well, maybe it's not your fuck-up — maybe you planned for it all along.'

'I can't believe you'd think—'

'Shut up,' King interrupts, knowing he has his handler in the palm of his hand. 'Again, I don't care. I'm coming back anyway. I'm gonna continue taking jobs, because I know they help good people and screw over bad people. It's dawning on me that maybe that's not the case for the other operatives, but there's nothing I can do about that.'

'What the hell are you talking about?'

'You know.'

All quiet.

Lars asks, 'You think we give you the gigs that are morally pure because we know your conscience wouldn't allow you to do the other work?'

'That's not what I *think*,' King says. 'It's what I know.'

Lars doesn't confirm it. He doesn't deny it, either.

'It's a messy world,' King goes on. 'I'm not gonna put on rose-tinted glasses — I'm too jaded for that. Bad shit needs to happen to prevent worse shit from happening. I get it. But *my* work helps people, and everyone keeps telling me I'm the best at it, so I'm going to keep doing it. Whether you betrayed me or not.'

No answer.

'I didn't betray you,' Lars says softly. 'But you'll never believe me.'

'It doesn't matter if I believe you. Here's the deal — I'm coming back, and we'll carry on: business as usual. I'll keep putting my life on the line for you. I'll save people who need saving. I'll kill people who need killing. And then at some point, when I'm tired of it all, I'll walk away.'

Lars doesn't respond.

'I always dreaded the day I'd have to make that choice,' King says, 'because I knew I might be signing my own death warrant. It makes sense — I wouldn't blame you if you didn't want me walking around as a civilian with state secrets in my head. But now I know that if I want out, and you come for me, I'll be able to handle it. So this is my offer.

'I'll keep doing the work for whoever your boss is, because *my* work is good and right. When I finally feel like my heart's no longer in it — whether that's a year, three years, five years from now — I'll bail. You won't try to stop me, because you know what will happen if you do. I'll go on to live my own life on my own terms. Is that understood?'

'Yes,' Lars says without hesitation. 'That's understood.'

'And Lars?'

'Yeah?'

'Enzo Navarro knew my name.'

A deafening silence.

'I didn't want it to happen,' Lars says softly, finally dropping the nuclear bomb of truth. 'It was a decision from the very top. It's been reversed. I swear on my life.'

King says nothing.

Lars can't handle the silence, and his walls come down. His voice is whisper-quiet. 'Why are you coming back if you knew?'

'Because the work is more important than my life,' King says. 'And if it happens again, I'll cave your fucking throat in. That's a promise.'

He hears Lars trying to suppress the noise of a panicked swallow. 'Understood. I'm sorry—'

'Save it,' King says, and kills the call.

He tosses the phone across the cargo compartment to the loadmaster, then settles back into his seat for the flight home.

He meant what he said. He knows he's the best in the world at what he does, and no matter the extent of the betrayals from above, he still believes deeply in his work. The day he doesn't, he's gone, and his time in South America has convinced him that no one can stop him from walking. The idea used to scare him; it no longer does.

Whatever they throw at him, he'll handle it.

Before this, he half-expected to undertake covert operations until he perished on a mission. He considered it an inevitability, part of the deal he signed up for. It's why he lives in the moment, never settling for anything less than his absolute best: because he's keenly aware that his days are numbered.

Now he's certain that one day he'll get out. He wants to serve his country; he no longer wants to die for it. Not when those at the very top are willing to throw him under the bus on the slightest whim. He's going back not for them, but for the thousands of innocents he's already saved, and the thousands more he can protect by doing his duty. The morality of those passing down the orders isn't relevant. What matters is the end result, and he's seen first-hand the good he's done. He isn't a politician or a bureaucrat or a strategist.

He's an elite killer with a conscience.

So he'll continue to kill the scum of the earth, save the victims who've done no wrong, and when he determines his time is up, he'll disappear into civilian life.

And then?

After he's free?

Maybe I'll do some wandering, he thinks.

Maybe I'll help some people of my own accord.

The vigilante life calls for him.

One day, he'll answer.

MORE LORE COMING SOON...

BOOKS BY MATT ROGERS

THE DANTE JACOBY SERIES

Be Somebody (Book 1)

Double Life (Book 2)

THE JASON KING SERIES

Isolated (Book 1)

Imprisoned (Book 2)

Reloaded (Book 3)

Betrayed (Book 4)

Corrupted (Book 5)

Hunted (Book 6)

THE JASON KING FILES

Cartel (Book 1)

Warrior (Book 2)

Savages (Book 3)

THE WILL SLATER SERIES

Wolf (Book 1)

Lion (Book 2)

Bear (Book 3)

Lynx (Book 4)

Bull (Book 5)

Hawk (Book 6)

THE KING & SLATER SERIES

Weapons (Book 1)

Contracts (Book 2)

Ciphers (Book 3)

Outlaws (Book 4)

Ghosts (Book 5)

Sharks (Book 6)

Messiahs (Book 7)

Hunters (Book 8)

Fathers (Book 9)

Tyrants (Book 10)

Monsters (Book 11)

Rogues (Book 12)

Legends (Book 13)

Smugglers (Book 14)

Daggers (Book 15)

Heroes (Book 16)

THE LORE OF KING & SLATER SERIES

Recruited (Book 1)

Thin Air (Book 2)

LYNX SHORTS

Blood Money (Book 1)

BLACK FORCE SHORTS

The Victor (Book 1)

The Chimera (Book 2)

WHAT'S NEXT?

I'm thrilled to announce my next project in the King & Slater Universe:

THE NEW GUARD
Book 1 of the Tyrell Slater Series

Nine years in the future, 24-year-old Tyrell Slater struggles to navigate a deeply changed world.

The rapid acceleration of technological progress has crippled society in unthinkable ways. Weaponising behavioural data, implementing mass surveillance, relentlessly pushing fast food and pills until the majority of the population is irreversibly trapped in a prison of addiction: it's all part of the plan.

Someone wanted this, and they're winning.
They're tearing the world apart.

An adult Tyrell must grapple with the responsibility he feels toward his fellow man, having inherited an intense compassion passed down by his mentor and de facto father, Will Slater.

THE NEW GUARD will feature **Jason King**, **Violetta LaFleur**, an eleven-year-old **Jason King Jr.**, and **Alexis Diaz** — all vastly changed by the progression of time.

I can't wait to write this new series for you.

Visit amazon.com/author/mattrogers23 and press **"Follow"** to be automatically notified when **THE NEW GUARD** releases.

Want more from Matt Rogers?

Watch or listen to my podcast, **"Heroic Traits,"** where I
break down life lessons from my novels:
https://linktr.ee/heroictraits

Follow me on Facebook:
https://www.facebook.com/mattrogersbooks

Follow me on Instagram:
https://www.instagram.com/mattrogersauthor

If you enjoyed the book, make sure to leave a review! Your
feedback means everything to me, and encourages me to
deliver more books as soon as I can.

Stay tuned.

Join the Reader's Group and get a free 200-page book by Matt Rogers!

Sign up for a free copy of '**BLOOD MONEY**'.

Meet Ruby Nazarian, a government operative for a clandestine initiative known only as Lynx. She's in Monaco to infiltrate the entourage of Aaron Wayne, a real estate tycoon on the precipice of dipping his hands into blood money. She charms her way aboard the magnate's superyacht, but everyone seems suspicious of her, and as the party ebbs onward she prepares for war...

Maybe she's paranoid.

Maybe not.

Just click here.

ABOUT THE AUTHOR

Matt Rogers grew up in Melbourne, Australia as a voracious reader, relentlessly devouring thrillers and mysteries in his spare time. Now, he writes full-time. His novels are action-packed and fast-paced. Dive into the Jason King Series to get started with his collection.

Visit his website:

www.mattrogersbooks.com

Visit his Amazon page:

amazon.com/author/mattrogers23